The automatic door buzzed, and Gianna summoned a pleasant smile, only to have it freeze with shock at the sight of the tall broad-shouldered man entering the boutique

His powerful frame appeared no less imposing than she remembered, and his dark hair gleamed, emphasizing broad-boned facial features, a strong jaw, wide cheekbones, the Mediterranean skin tone, and eyes so dark they appeared almost black.

Raúl. Ex-lover, estranged husband…and a man she had fervently hoped never to see again. *Dear heaven. What was he doing here?*

She lingered a little too long on his mouth, the sensual curve revived a host of memories she fought hard to control. Vivid, primitive…so much so, she could almost *feel* the touch of his lips, the wicked sweep of his tongue.

Oh, God. The silent despairing groan remained locked in her throat. *Don't go there.* It took all her effort to tilt her head a little and summon a wry smile.

She glimpsed a muscle bunch above the edge of his jaw and felt a moment of satisfaction as she enjoyed the small visible sign of his tension, too.

"What brings you here Raúl?"

One eyebrow lifted in cynical query. "You."

All about the author...
Helen Bianchin

HELEN BIANCHIN grew up in New Zealand, an only child possessed by a vivid imagination and a love for reading. After four years of legal-secretarial work, Helen embarked on a working holiday in Australia where she met her Italian-born husband, a tobacco sharefarmer in far north Queensland. His command of English was pitiful, and her command of Italian was nil. Fun? Oh yes! So, too, was being flung into cooking for workers immediately after marriage, stringing tobacco and living in primitive conditions.

It was a few years later when Helen, her husband and their daughter returned to New Zealand, settled in Auckland and added two sons to their family. Encouraged by friends to recount anecdotes of her years as a tobacco sharefarmer's wife living in an Italian community, Helen began setting words on paper and her first novel was published in 1975.

Creating interesting characters and telling their stories remains as passionate a challenge for Helen as it was in the beginning of her writing career.

Spending time with family, reading and watching movies are high on Helen's list of pleasures. An animal lover, Helen says her Maltese terrier and two Birman cats regard her study as much theirs as hers.

Helen Bianchin

PUBLIC MARRIAGE, PRIVATE SECRETS

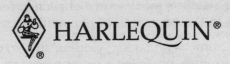

HARLEQUIN®

TORONTO • NEW YORK • LONDON
AMSTERDAM • PARIS • SYDNEY • HAMBURG
STOCKHOLM • ATHENS • TOKYO • MILAN • MADRID
PRAGUE • WARSAW • BUDAPEST • AUCKLAND

Recycling programs
for this product may
not exist in your area.

ISBN-13: 978-0-373-12945-4

PUBLIC MARRIAGE, PRIVATE SECRETS

First North American Publication 2010.

Copyright © 2010 by Helen Bianchin.

This is a work of fiction. Names, characters, places and incidents are either the product of the author's imagination or are used fictitiously, and any resemblance to actual persons, living or dead, business establishments, events or locales is entirely coincidental.

This edition published by arrangement with Harlequin Books S.A.

For questions and comments about the quality of this book please contact us at Customer_eCare@Harlequin.ca.

® and TM are trademarks of the publisher. Trademarks indicated with ® are registered in the United States Patent and Trademark Office, the Canadian Trade Marks Office and in other countries.

www.eHarlequin.com

Printed in U.S.A.

PUBLIC MARRIAGE, PRIVATE SECRETS

CHAPTER ONE

Gianna exited her Main Beach apartment block and walked the short distance to where the Pacific ocean's incoming tide brought rolling waves crashing gently into shore. The early morning sky was pale blue and cloudless, the spring sunshine promising warmth.

Change is *good*, Gianna assured herself, as she stepped onto the pale golden sand.

Although *why* she'd chosen a jog along the beach instead of her customary session in a local gym wasn't something she was prepared to examine in any depth.

The phase of the moon? A restless night due to intrusive dreams?

Whatever... Being outside in fresh sea air held an appeal, and here she was, ready to banish any lingering demons.

Forty minutes of exercise, coffee-to-go to kick-start the day, before returning to her apartment to shower, breakfast, dress and leave for work.

Bellissima, the luxury gift boutique she owned in one of the Gold Coast's trendiest suburbs, had gained a favourable reputation for its mix of imported and local stock. Exquisite scented candles, beautiful soaps, ornamental glassware, small sculptures whose graceful lines in crystal, ebony and silver drew attention. Embroidered napkins on fine

Irish linen, silk pillow-covers, quality gift cards were just some of the wares she offered for sale.

Fate had provided the opportunity for her to purchase the boutique almost a year after being employed as manager during the owner's absence. Now, two years on, a new shop-fit, quality stock, a twice-yearly catalogue, and turnover had increased dramatically.

Life, Gianna reflected as she broke into a jog along the tightly packed sand, was good. At the age of twenty-eight she owned a successful business, an apartment, and she had carved out a satisfactory existence.

Moved on, she assured herself as a faint sea breeze caressed her skin, from the break-up of her brief marriage to the powerful Spaniard she'd met four years ago at a party during a holiday in Mallorca.

Raúl Velez-Saldaña.

In his late thirties, tall, dark, ruggedly attractive…and dangerous to any woman's peace of mind.

Who could resist him? What woman would *want* to?

One look was all it had taken for her to melt into an ignominious puddle at his feet. Well, not quite.

She'd fought him at first, then herself. Knowing even then if she succumbed she'd be *lost*…completely, utterly.

Gianna shivered despite the increasing warmth of the sun as she headed south along the shoreline.

What they had shared had been more than just sex. It had been intimacy at its zenith…intense, mesmeric, *primitive.* Six perfect months together, *living* in the moment, unable to bear being apart.

A time when Raúl had clocked up air miles as if they were nothing, and she'd used allocated holiday time and sick leave to meet him *wherever…*

Until the moment she had agreed to relocate to Madrid and move into his luxurious apartment in residential Salamanca. Dear heaven, the *life* she'd shared with him...

A slip, just *one* gap, where a differing time zone had ensured she slept during a long international flight to Sydney, to attend her brother Ben's wedding, and she had missed taking a low-dosage contraceptive pill.

She vividly recalled the day when she had first suspected she might be pregnant. Worse, the precise time the pregnancy test had registered positive...a test she'd taken *three* times within forty-eight hours to ensure there was no mistake.

How she'd agonised for days before telling him. The calm manner in which he had received the news. Even more controlled had been his solution...*marriage*.

Her spontaneous, 'Because...?' hadn't brought the avowal of love she'd longed to hear.

Somehow his, 'No child of mine will be born out of wedlock,' had failed to compensate.

The abortion route wasn't an alternative she'd been able to condone or consider. Nor his insistence that marriage was the *only* option.

Yet what had been the alternative? A choice of returning to Australia and raising the child alone? Fighting a custody battle with Raúl...one he'd surely win? Or marriage?

At the end of the day...*days*, she amended, when she'd tortured herself in order to reach the *right* decision...it had been no contest.

Raúl's widowed mother's delight and genuine blessing had provided the persuasive factor. A child *deserved* to have a father in its life, *family*.

Something which struck a chord with Gianna, for her own mother had been killed in an auto accident years ago. Her father had met someone else, relocated to Paris and remarried. There was a step-family now. Gianna rarely saw them…just a series of e-mails, attachments with photographs, and the occasional phone call.

Ben, her brother, to whom she remained close, kept in weekly contact via phone and regular e-mail.

Girlfriends…the genuine kind with whom she maintained contact…were few, and located in different countries in the world.

Consequently she'd opted for a new beginning in a different locale from Sydney, the city in which she'd been born, educated and employed.

Another state—Queensland, with its sub-tropical climate, beautiful beaches and Australia's tourist mecca—had beckoned, and now, almost three years later, it felt like *home*.

Raúl had *cared* for her, this much she knew. So what if it hadn't been *love*? Care was *enough*…and who could predict what the future might hold?

Bittersweet words, Gianna reflected, given she'd suffered a miscarriage within seven weeks of becoming Gianna Velez-Saldaña.

It had been a time when she'd desperately wanted, *needed* his comfort. At night she had lain awake, long after he slept, craving his touch. *More*, so much more, than simply being pulled close and held securely in his arms.

Grief, sorrow…dammit, *hormones*, had succeeded in providing an altered reasoning. Together with the sweetly delivered but nonetheless heartless words from Sierra, one of Raúl's ex-lovers, who had essayed it might have been prudent to wait until closer to the child's birth before rushing into marriage.

From there, it had been downhill all the way, with Raúl spending more time in his city office, caught up with meetings, leaving before she woke most mornings and frequently missing dinner for some seemingly valid reason or another, occasionally arriving home long after she'd retired to bed.

Communication between them had become reduced to the perfunctory. Polite exchanges in private, while maintaining the required image in public.

The explosive meltdown had come when she had called his cellphone one evening while he was on a business trip in Argentina and Sierra had answered, almost *purring* with delight as she'd revealed that '*now* is not a good time… *comprende?*' As if the implication might be misunderstood, Sierra had sharpened the verbal barb with unvarnished clarity. 'Raúl is filling the spa-bath. Need I say I'm about to join him?' And cut the connection.

After the numbness had come anger, followed by a crying jag…then she'd calmly packed her bags and called a taxi to take her to the airport, where she'd caught the first available flight home.

Old news, she remonstrated in self-castigation.

She'd moved on, sought solace in the familiar, ensured a new life for herself…a successful one…and rebuilt her confidence and self-respect.

The cry of a lonely seagull rent the early morning quietness, providing a distraction, and Gianna watched the bird's graceful glide to settle at the water's edge. Its red beak dug into the wet sand and emerged with a tidbit…a baby sand-crab, perhaps? Then, apparently delighted with its find, it sent up a shrill, keening cry which soon brought several gulls to the scene.

Apartment towers lined the Esplanade—tall concrete sentinels of varying architectural design bearing exotic names.

Already the incoming tide was beginning to swell with white-crested waves that broke and rolled gently into shore…a precursor of bigger waves ideal for surfing.

Within minutes she changed direction and headed up the slight sandy incline to the boardwalk, where she crossed the road to a pavement café and ordered a latte to go.

Already several tables were occupied, as holiday-makers sought an early breakfast beneath colourful shade umbrellas.

It was almost seven-thirty when Gianna entered her apartment, and she stripped off her clothes, showered, dressed, ate fresh fruit and yoghurt, then caught up her laptop and bag, filched her keys from the side-table adjacent to the front door, and took the lift down to the basement car park.

A short drive brought her to an upmarket complex, unique in design, with its arched sails reaching skywards, housing various boutiques of which Bellisima was one, and a faint smile softened her mouth as she took a moment to check the window display.

Visually attractive, she conceded as she bent low to unlock the front doors. Perhaps she could replace the pewter vase with the crystal conch-shell, add a collection of silk flowers. Exchange the stunning beaten silver platter with the pair of multi-coloured glass birds.

The gift boutique was so much *hers*, with the art of display reflecting her excellent taste, her instinctive knack of placing unusual items together to draw maximum attention to the mirrored walls with their glass shelving.

Each item gleamed beneath the fluorescent lighting, the colours like fine jewels in their brilliance, and she allowed herself a moment of pride before crossing to the service desk, where she prepared for the start of a new business day.

Morning trade was fairly brisk, with purchases made and those chosen as gifts wrapped with exquisite care, earning delighted gratitude from each customer.

Gianna derived immense pleasure in providing warm and friendly service. Something which had earned her a loyal and select client base.

She'd made the boutique her *life*, constantly searching for unusual items to attract her customers. She also provided a comprehensive catalogue, and maintained a constantly updated Web page to showcase upcoming imports and deliveries.

The fact she'd achieved it on her own, with loan funds from the bank, was a source of pride. Monthly amounts paid by Raúl directly into a separate bank account remained untouched.

Work had become all-involving, filling her waking hours. Her focus was *now*, and the immediate future.

There were a few *good* friends, but, while she occasionally socialised, she didn't date. Dinner and pleasant conversation didn't include an automatic agreement for consensual sex at evening's end. At least not in her book.

She tried…she really did. Her friends meant well. They wanted to see her happy, content, with a regular man in her life who *cared*.

'He's wonderful—a real gentleman' didn't hold true, she had discovered to her cost.

'You'll adore him, he's so charming…' Uh-huh—if you enjoyed the obsequious type.

No matter how well-intentioned, their efforts failed. Or perhaps *she* failed…for *moving on* from Raúl wasn't happening.

He was *there*, his physical image so easily summoned to mind she almost expected to see him, and occasionally felt the breath catch in her throat whenever she sighted a tall, broad-shouldered male whose stance at first glance seemed achingly familiar. Followed by a heart-lurching few seconds when everything within her peripheral vision froze into a fixed tableau…until she glimpsed his profile and saw the face of a stranger, and her personal world returned to its normal kilter.

Oh, for heaven's sake, she chastised in self-castigation. There was work to do. Stock to arrange. Deliveries to check. And her clientele. *A business to run.*

Busy was good. A steady flow of people wanting assistance ensured there was little time in which to think or reflect, and Gianna welcomed Annaliese, the part-time assistant who helped out in the boutique from ten-thirty to four, seven days a week.

It was an employment arrangement that worked well, and had done so for the past two years.

Attractive, intelligent, sunny-tempered, with a droll sense of humour, Annaliese was a superb salesperson and, importantly, dedicated.

'Hi. One double-shot skim latte for *madame.*'

Delivering coffee, hot and strong, had become a welcome habit Annaliese had initiated during the first week of her employment.

'Thanks.' Gianna's gratitude was genuine, and Annaliese offered a warm smile as she took the capped takeaway cup to the small back room. 'Busy morning?'

The day brought several customers into the boutique. There were the serious buyers, and those who merely browsed, as well as a few regulars.

It was almost five when Gianna checked the sales register. The recorded total revealed a satisfactorily high figure…sufficient to warrant ordering replacement stock. Something she'd tend to prior to closing time.

A faint prickle began at her nape and slipped down her spine as she cut the phone connection to her supplier with bare minutes to spare before she was due to walk out through the door.

The electronic door buzzed, and she summoned a pleasant smile...only to have it freeze with shock at the sight of the man entering the boutique.

His powerful frame appeared no less imposing than she remembered, and his dark hair gleamed beneath the artificial lighting, emphasising broad-boned facial features, a strong jaw, wide cheekbones, the Mediterranean skin tone...and eyes so dark they appeared almost black.

Raúl.

Ex-lover, estranged husband...and a man she had fervently hoped never to see again.

Dear heaven. *What was he doing here?*

For a startling moment she was flung back to a time when her life had been everything she could want it to be.

Until it had all fallen apart in those wretched few months following her miscarriage, when the pain of grief had wrought such havoc.

He'd phoned, and when she had refused to take his calls he'd arrived on her doorstep, demanding she return with him to Madrid.

Except she'd stood her ground, wanting time and space alone...and he'd left, assuring her the next move had to be *hers*.

'Nothing to say, Gianna?'

The slightly accented drawl curled round her nerve-ends and brought her crashing back to reality as she took in his etched features.

Eyes as dark as sin, with tiny lines fanning out from the edges. Vertical grooves bracketing each cheek, which seemed slightly deeper and more clearly defined.

She lingered a little too long on his mouth... The sensual curve revived a host of memories she fought hard to control. Vivid, primitive…so much so she could almost *feel* the touch of his lips, the wicked sweep of his tongue.

Oh, God. The silent despairing groan remained locked in her throat. *Don't go there.*

It took all her effort to tilt her head a little and summon a wry smile.

'What would you have me offer? *Hello, how are you?* seems…' She paused deliberately.

'Inadequate?'

'Incredibly banal,' Gianna concluded, and saw his eyes darken.

'Now, there's an interesting word.'

She glimpsed a muscle bunch above the edge of his jaw and felt a moment of satisfaction as she enjoyed the small visible sign of his tension.

Even though she wore high heels Raúl still towered above her, and she tilted her head in order to align her eyes with his.

'What brings you here?'

'Australia? The Gold Coast in particular?' he drawled, and she swept an arm to encompass the boutique.

'*Here.*'

One eyebrow lifted in cynical query. 'To see you.'

'A phone call would have taken care of whatever you have to say.'

'If you chose to take my call.'

Would she have? She still had his name on her caller register. So she could pick up or ignore if he rang. He hadn't, but she'd felt the need to have the option.

'I can't imagine anything being sufficiently important to warrant your personal appearance.'

He looked at her carefully, examining her slender form… more slender than he remembered. Pale features beneath the skilled touch of light make-up, the almost undetectable shadows beneath her brilliant blue eyes. The deep-beating pulse at the base of her throat.

Not so calm beneath her projected persona, Raúl detected with a degree of satisfaction.

'No?'

She couldn't quite restrain the faint edge to her voice. 'There's nothing you could say that I want to hear.'

At that moment the door buzzer sounded, and it took her a few seconds to ignore the silent *as if I need this now?* before she turned towards the entrance.

'Excuse me? Are you still open?'

Raúl inclined his head towards Gianna in silent query, admiring her switch to polite composure as she summoned a smile and moved forward to greet the customer.

'Is there anything I can help you with?'

'The large red bowl in the window display. As soon as I saw it I knew it would be perfect.'

'Exquisite, isn't it?' Gianna relayed with professional ease. 'Imported Venetian glass.' She crossed to the display and carefully removed the item. The ticket price was clearly visible and, although expensive, the woman didn't hesitate.

'I'll take it.'

Gianna produced a warm smile. 'Is it a gift? Would you like it gift-wrapped?'

'If it's no trouble.'

'It'll be a pleasure.' It took only minutes to extract the appropriate box and carefully package the bowl, select wrapping paper, ribbon and effect an elegant bow.

With deft movements the task was completed, credit card swiped, a signature attached to the slip, and a very satisfied customer expressed gratitude as Gianna accompanied her to the entry, wished her good evening, then carefully locked the glass doors.

'Do whatever needs to be done, then we'll leave.'

'*We?*' Gianna queried with deliberate emphasis as she crossed to the sales counter. 'I'm not going anywhere with you.'

'I think you will.' His voice held a dangerous silkiness, and her eyes sharpened into deep blue shards.

The thought of sharing time with him and pretending to make polite conversation was the last thing she wanted to do.

'Give me one reason why I should.'

He didn't prevaricate or lead into it gently…just a single word, aware that it would get her attention as no other would. 'Teresa.'

Gianna's eyes widened, only to cloud with concern at the mention of his mother. For it had been Teresa Velez-Saldaña who had welcomed her son's lover with affection, fondly sanctioned the marriage and wept genuine tears at the loss of their child.

A very special woman, who'd kept wise counsel when Gianna had left Madrid, and who'd chosen to remain in contact at regular intervals…warm, quirky missives despatched in a continued bid to maintain their close bond, including an open invitation for Gianna to visit at any time.

Letters to which Gianna had responded with caution at first, managing to overcome her initial reserve only as the months passed with no mention of Raúl's name.

Her stomach clenched in pain at the thought Teresa might be ill, injured or…heaven forbid…worse.

'No.'

'No *what*?' Gianna demanded trenchantly, unbearably irked that he still retained the ability to read her mind. Somehow she'd imagined, *hoped*, she had acquired an impenetrable façade in the past few years.

Apparently not.

For a long moment she simply looked at him, silently daring him to shift his gaze. Except he didn't, and she became conscious of the pulse at the base of her throat kicking into a quickened thud.

Every cell in her body seemed to blaze into life, and she hated that he *knew*.

'*Tell me*, dammit.'

His eyes darkened measurably. 'A few weeks ago Teresa was diagnosed with inoperable cancer.'

For a few seemingly long seconds she was lost for words. 'Teresa made no mention of illness in any of her letters,' she managed at last—for affection, trust and mutual respect had developed into a genuinely warm friendship between both women. 'I'm so sorry.'

'Yes, I believe you are.' His eyes held her own, and she almost swayed at the intensity of his gaze. 'Enough,' he continued quietly, 'to fulfil one of her dearest wishes?'

She schooled her voice to remain calm in spite of the premonition that she wasn't going to like what he intended to say. 'If it's possible,' she managed with instinctive caution.

'Teresa has requested the pleasure of your company.'

Gianna froze, the colour leaching from her cheeks, revealing starkly pale features as she contrived to control the onset of nerves threatening to play havoc with her emotions.

'In Madrid?' An unnecessary query, when she already knew the answer before he could confirm it.

'Initially.'

CHAPTER TWO

MADRID.

The city where Raúl resided and ruled his late father's multibillion-dollar consortium.

A silent scream rose and died in her throat at the mere thought of seeing him, pretending politeness whenever he visited to spend time with Teresa.

As he would…often.

She couldn't do it.

Amend that… She didn't *want* to be anywhere near Raúl. She especially didn't want to be placed in a position over which she had little control.

'You can't be serious?

His eyes held hers, compellingly intent. 'Very serious.'

A host of conflicting thoughts swirled through her brain.

If she agreed…

Are you *insane?*

She had a business to run. She couldn't just pick up and leave at a moment's notice.

'A few weeks of your time, Gianna,' Raúl pursued, his voice dangerously soft. 'Is that too much to ask?'

Her first instinct was to offer a resounding *yes*…even as her head reeled at the mechanics involved.

She'd need to appoint Annaliese as interim manager, employ another staff member, organise stock, orders...

A silent groan rose and died in her throat.

Oh, hell, why was she giving it consideration? The whole thing was impossible.

Raúl caught a glimpse of each fleeting emotion on her expressive features and was able to divine every one of them.

'Teresa looks upon you as her daughter,' he offered quietly. 'Irrespective of our estrangement. There are a few special items...heirlooms...she wants to gift to you in person.'

No. The negation rose and died in her throat.

Please don't do this to me.

'I couldn't possibly accept them.'

'Why not?'

'They should belong to you,' she said quickly. Too quickly. The words tumbled without thought. 'Your family. Your wife.'

Oh, God, what had she said?

With a sense of horrified dismay she saw one eyebrow slant with a hint of humour. 'You *are* my wife,' Raúl reminded her silkily. 'Or had you forgotten we're still legally married?'

Forgotten? How could she forget, when never a day went past when his image didn't come to mind? Or night...when he managed to invade her dreams.

'You can't expect me to agree,' she managed at last.

'There is a valid reason why you can't?'

Several, she longed to fling, truly torn as she mentally weighed her loyalty to a genuinely kind woman who had gifted unconditional support at a time when she'd needed it most.

To give in would mean revisiting painful memories, not

the least of which took the form of the indomitable man who now stood before her.

A man whose physical impact affected every nerve in her body, heightening tension to an electrifying degree.

Three years, she agonised silently, and *nothing had changed*.

'There's a lover you're reluctant to leave?'

She didn't know whether to laugh or cry at his assumption. *As if.* Any man she'd encountered after Raúl didn't come close, for there was no spark, no quickening of her pulse...*nothing*.

Yet how many lovers had *he* taken since she'd walked out on their marriage? Sierra Montefiore...had *she* quickly resumed her former place as one of them?

The mere thought sent a shaft of pain arrowing through her body.

'Yes,' she revealed with unaccustomed flippancy, knowing it to be false...unless Jazz, the black-and-white moggy she'd adopted from an animal rescue centre, counted. Male, he curled up on her bed every night, his warm, furry feline body a welcome comfort.

Raúl's eyes darkened, then narrowed a little so fleetingly she almost missed it.

'I'm sure he can exist without you for a few weeks,' he drawled with dispassionate coolness.

Gianna pretended to consider the possibility. 'Doubtful.' Jazz would protest volubly at being deposited in a boarding cattery, and probably disdain gifting her his affection for days on her return. The little fluff-ball possessed a territorial personality...the apartment was *his*. Anyone who entered was duly inspected, reluctant approval given or denied, and thereafter subject to slit-eyed feline observance.

'Yes or no, Gianna.'

She cast him a disparaging look. 'In case you haven't

done your homework, I run this boutique with one part-time member of staff. Even if I wanted to, I couldn't leave at a moment's notice.'

'I wasn't aware I'd asked that of you.'

'Really? The man who snaps his fingers and every employed minion jumps to obey your command?'

Amusement lifted the edges of his mouth. 'You are not one of my minions.'

'Hallelujah.'

'Have dinner with me, and we'll discuss whatever arrangements you need to make.'

'I don't recall saying yes, yet.'

'You didn't need to.' The dry tones held a degree of mockery…something she chose to ignore. There was the temptation to stand her ground, except it would prove an exercise in futility.

Without a further word, she crossed to the serving counter and dealt with the sales register, where it took only minutes to check folding money, credit slips, assemble the cash float. When she was done, she dimmed the overhead lights, collected her bag, engaged security and indicated they should leave.

Raúl loomed large at her side as they walked towards the escalator, and she was all too aware of his close proximity not to mention how he affected her.

It wasn't *fair* to feel like this after an absence of three years. Hateful to be transported back to a time when she'd *lived* for him…only him. Even *thinking* about him had made her happy, and as soon as he'd appeared it had been all she could do not to break into a quickened pace and leap into his arms.

The way he'd laugh and hold her close, nuzzle the soft curve at the edge of her neck…then cover her mouth with his own in a kiss that reached down into her soul.

Heaven, she reflected as she stepped off the escalator, feeling momentarily bereft that what they'd once shared had been lost.

'I'm staying at the resort directly opposite.' Raúl indicated as he joined her. 'We'll eat there.'

'I have plans for the evening.' *Some plans,* she reiterated silently. Drive home, change, feed Jazz, make herself something to eat, watch television, then call it a night.

He spared her a level look. 'Postpone them.'

Gianna turned to confront him. 'And if I choose not to?'

'Do you particularly want to indulge in a verbal fencing match?'

He was standing too close, and she was suddenly all too aware of the subtle aroma of his cologne, light with musky undertones. Indisputably *his*, as if crafted especially for him.

It stirred her senses and awakened too many sensitive nerve-endings for her peace of mind.

Raúl's eyes narrowed fractionally, almost as if he *knew*, and it irked unbearably…so much so she raked his tall frame from head to foot and back again with slow deliberation.

'Let's get one thing straight.' She took a deep calming breath. 'If I agree, it'll be on my terms,' she qualified as her eyes seared his own with unblinking determination. 'It'll take days, possibly a week, for me to organise staff, contact my clientele, suppliers, ensure there will be no hiccups with replacement stock arriving on time. When that's in place, I'll take the first available flight to Madrid, arrange hotel accommodation, and inform you of my arrival.' There was more, and she delivered the words with precise care. 'Meantime, I suggest you return to Madrid.'

'That's it?' he queried silkily.

'Yes.'

He regarded her with dispassionate imperturbability. 'No.'

'No—*what*?'

'We'll return together in my private jet, and hotel accommodation isn't an option.'

'That's *ridiculous*.'

Only a fool would refuse to travel in the maximum comfort afforded by luxury fittings which included a lounge that converted easily into a working office, a bedroom with en suite bathroom...and being served by a personal in-flight attendant.

Except it meant endless air hours secluded in Raúl's company something she'd do almost anything to avoid.

'I'd prefer to take a commercial flight.'

For a long moment he regarded her with lazy appreciation, and there was nothing she could do to still the increased tempo of her heart...or the faint shivery sensation feathering her fine body hairs.

'Teresa has a full complement of medical staff on hand. The villa in Mallorca is large, and she insists you stay there as her guest.'

Mallorca? 'I don't think...'

'Determined to fight me on every issue, Gianna?'

'You expect anything less?'

'Shall we call a temporary truce?'

She looked at him carefully. 'It's been a long day. I have work to do and calls to make.'

'In which case you can eat and leave. An hour, Gianna... or less.'

Reluctance vied with determination to prove she was immune to him. A distinct untruth, if ever there was one, but she refused to concede him so much as a glimmer of satisfaction. *You can do this*, she vaunted silently.

She effected a seemingly careless shrug. 'I guess so.'

Raúl spared her a musing glance and caught the faint air of tension apparent in her demeanour. She reminded him of a gazelle, uncertain whether to trust or flee.

With good reason, he admitted silently as he indicated the escalator at the eastern end of the spacious forecourt.

For flee she certainly would if she suspected there was another reason for Teresa's request. One infinitely more precious than the personal gift of a few heirlooms, or the pleasure of spending time in Gianna's company.

The fervent hope Teresa held for a reconciliation between her son and the young woman he'd taken as his wife.

A young woman so well matched to his needs it seemed almost a crime for the marriage to have fallen apart.

Dusk was falling as they crossed the overhead pedestrian walkway to the popular low-level resort. Already streetlights shone, and in the distance the tall concrete sentinels harbouring luxury apartments bore illumination against a darkening skyscape.

The expansive resort foyer, with its plush oriental carpet squares and large comfortable chairs, bore a Caribbean air which extended to a wide marble staircase leading down to ground level. A magnificent waterfall cascaded into a decorative pool, and beyond huge thick plate glass lay an extensive swimming pool, with an island bar fronting on to a sandy foreshore and the sparkling blue waters of the Pacific Ocean.

The *à la carte* restaurant held a small clientele as the *maître d'* led the way to a table by the window, saw them seated, and summoned the drinks steward.

Raúl's presence garnered discreet attention especially from the women present. Not surprising, Gianna reluctantly conceded, given his attractive broad-boned Mediterranean features.

There was something that set him apart from his contemporaries. An elusive ruthlessness lay beneath the sophisticated exterior, meshing an inherent masculine vitality with latent sensuality. Add an animalistic sense of power, and the combination proved electric…dramatic.

Fine tailoring, handcrafted shoes, the faint glimpse of a Rolex gracing his wrist, merely showcased a man whose presence was equally dynamic in anything he chose to wear…or not.

As she could attest to…and she hated the sensation that shook her slender form as an image of his splendid body unadorned rose to taunt her.

The broad shoulders, superb musculature, lean waist and hips, tight butt, long powerful legs. Awesome…in every area.

She recalled how it felt to be held close to him, the faint muskiness of aroused male combining with his elusive cologne…*oh, God,* his skilled touch with his mouth, tongue, fingers, as he sought out every sensitive pulse, each erotic nerve-end in a bid to escalate her emotions to fever-pitch…

Stop!

For a wild moment she imagined she'd screamed the word out loud.

What was wrong with her?

Somehow she managed a seemingly polite façade as the drinks steward approached and offered a formal greeting and presented Raúl with the wine list.

'We have an excellent selection. Do you have a particular preference, or would you prefer me to offer a suggestion?'

Dark eyes captured her own. 'Gianna?'

It was easy to defer, and she did so with a polite smile. 'You choose.'

He did…a mild red, well-known as one of Australia's finest vintages.

'Mineral water—still,' she added, and earned Raúl's faintly arched eyebrow.

'The need for a clear head?'

'An aversion to drink-driving.'

'Wise.'

She summoned a sweet smile as she accepted the proffered menu, and pretended to study the various selections while attempting to deal with a host of conflicting emotions.

It didn't make sense.

She was over him…had been for a while, she reiterated silently.

To the point of weighing up the need to initiate divorce. *Three years*… Even discounting the initial few months of separation, when she'd retreated into despair, sufficient time had elapsed to reach a decision.

So…*why* the nervous tension? Or the wildly beating pulse-rate that threatened to go off the Richter scale?

She couldn't be susceptible to him…*surely*?

The mere thought was untenable. *Impossible*.

She was unaware of her teeth worrying the soft swell of her lower lip or of the faint narrowing of Raúl's eyes as he caught the gesture.

'Shall we order?'

The thought of forking morsels of food in his presence held little appeal. Consequently she settled for an entree as a main, with a side salad, and declined dessert.

It was as he lifted his goblet of wine that she noticed a gleam of gold on his left hand, and her eyes widened in recognition of the unique handcrafted band she'd placed there on the day of their wedding.

He still wore it?

Why so surprised, when her own still graced *her* hand?

Admittedly transferred to her right hand. A wide bevelled gold band encrusted with diamonds. She had been morally unable to discard it while the marriage remained valid.

Gianna searched for something to say...and came up with nothing that made any sense.

You're looking well didn't cut it.

How is business these days? seemed ludicrous, given his consortium had inevitably diversified into areas she had little or no comprehension of, racking up millions in the process.

Failure and Raúl Velez-Saldaña did not equate.

He was a hard-hearted ruthless entrepreneur, well-respected for his uncanny ability to successfully manipulate and strategise, forging ahead with unfailing resolve when colleagues and adversaries chose to opt out.

Yet each acquisition was carefully and painstakingly researched, every possible angle examined to the *nth* degree.

She could recall the times she'd awakened alone in their bed in the late-night hours, only to find him closeted in his home office studying graphs and projections on-screen.

Then she would go to him, ease the tension in tight shoulder and neck muscles, and suggest he needed sleep... only to have him smile, press *save* and pull her onto his lap. *Sleep*, as such, had rarely happened for a while.

*Dear heaven...*why were such memories surfacing *now*?

It was madness. A brief moment of insanity she immediately banished to the nether regions of hell.

'I suggest you tell me precisely what Teresa will expect of me.' Her voice sounded calm, even to her own ears… amazing, given she was an emotional mess.

'The pleasure of your company. One-on-one time.' His eyes speared her own—dark, enigmatic. 'She occasionally lunches with a few close friends, and I imagine she will delight in having you join her.'

Not a difficult ask. She held his gaze, silently wishing it wasn't so hard to do so. 'I'll be happy to fit in with whatever Teresa wants me to do.'

A woman Gianna held in high esteem, whose compassion, genuine affection and loyalty had helped fill the void left by losing her own mother at a young age.

The only stumbling block was Raúl himself, for spending any time in his company would be *difficult*, to say the least.

Yet a few weeks wasn't a lifetime, she rationalised. Primarily, her purpose was to fulfil Teresa's wish to be able to say goodbye in person.

Time to focus on the prosaic…and she did it by forking delicate morsels of food without tasting a thing.

Soon the meal would conclude and she could leave, retrieve her car from the shopping complex and retreat to the sanctuary of her apartment.

If only it were that simple.

Yet *nothing* about the man seated opposite could be categorised as *simple*. For how was it possible for her to feel as if she'd been caught up in a sensual whirlpool when she'd vowed to hate him?

It didn't make sense.

So? a tiny voice taunted. *Why waste time and energy attempting to solve the impossible?*

Raúl ate with evident enjoyment, and she found it annoying that he could appear so totally at ease when she felt as if she was caught up in an emotional maelstrom.

'Perhaps you'd care to enlighten me about *your* life in the intervening three years?'

'Specifically?'

'Insignificant personal details.'

'Such as?'

Oh, spit it out, why don't you? 'Your current lover.'

His eyes darkened measurably, and she glimpsed a muscle bunch at the edge of his jaw. 'Do you particularly want to cover old ground?'

'Not really.' Amazing how much it still hurt. 'I think it's reasonable to ask if I'm likely to be confronted by a woman in your life.'

'That isn't a consideration.'

Which didn't answer the question.

'Sierra?'

'A brief testament to her superb acting and my poor judgement well before I met you,' Raúl insisted silkily. 'And never afterwards.'

It surprised her how much she wanted to believe him. Yet the evidence was stacked heavily against him.

It was a relief when the meal concluded. She declined coffee, then retrieved a few notes to cover her share and placed them on the table.

'You choose to insult me?'

His voice was silky soft and dangerous. Something Gianna elected to ignore.

'Not at all.' She stood to her feet, and felt a moment's reservation when Raúl followed suit. 'I imagine we'll be in touch?' she offered, with the utmost politeness.

She didn't wait for his answer as she turned from the table, acknowledging the *maître d'* with a faint smile as she exited the restaurant into the main lobby.

The sense of relief was enormous, and she was conscious of the click of her stiletto heels on the tiled floor as she crossed to the automatic front doors.

The concierge inclined his head as she passed through into the spacious courtyard, and she'd almost reached the overhead pedestrian bridge when Raúl joined her.

He had the tread of a cat, and she sent him a level look as she kept walking. 'We've already said goodnight.'

'I don't recall *goodnight* being mentioned.' His voice held drawled cynicism.

'How remiss of me,' Gianna said sweetly. *'Buenas noches.'*

Traffic flowed freely on the dual carriageway beneath them. In all probability patrons heading towards the parking facilities offered by the many restaurants situated in the immediate vicinity.

'There's no need for you to play the gentleman,' she voiced as they reached the upper level of the shopping complex. 'I'm perfectly capable of reaching my car unaided.'

'Of course you are.'

He followed her onto the escalator, and when she stepped onto ground level he accompanied her down to the underground parking area.

She ignored him and crossed to the bay containing her small Lexus sedan, released the remote locking mechanism, slid in behind the wheel and ignited the engine.

'Satisfied?'

Far from it, he admitted. But she would keep.

He removed a card from his pocket and handed it to her through the open window. 'My cellphone number.'

The overhead fluorescent lighting threw his features into shadow, making his expression difficult to define.

'Thanks.'

The window slid closed, and she lifted a hand in a polite wave as she sent the car towards the exit ramp.

With care she entered the stream of traffic, turned left towards the roundabout, then circled back along the southbound carriageway leading towards Main Beach.

It wasn't until she reached the solitude of her apartment that she allowed herself to relax, and she scooped up the fluff-ball patiently awaiting her arrival.

'Hi, there, gorgeous.' She stroked the soft fur beneath his chin. 'Miss me?'

His response was to curl his head into the palm of her hand as she made for the kitchen to feed him.

When he was happily eating, she removed her stilettos and crossed to her bedroom, where she discarded her clothes, showered. Then, attired in her night wear, she took a cup of tea into the room she'd converted into her home office, set up her laptop, and worked until Jazz leapt up onto the desk in protest.

'Yes, I know. Time to call it a night.'

She lifted both arms and stretched, felt the stiffness of neck and shoulder muscles, then saved her work, closed down, placed Jazz in his sleep basket and entered her bedroom.

It was late, much later than she usually chose to retire, and she slid beneath the bedcovers, switched off the bedside lamp…aware that within minutes the adorable fluff-ball would disdain his sleep basket, enter her room, and leap onto the foot of the bed, where he'd settle comfortably and remain until morning.

Raúl's disturbing image intruded, and she replayed the evening from the moment he entered the boutique until she left the underground car parking area. An hour and a half, that was all, yet she could recall every detail.

None of which aided an easy passage into restful sleep, and it didn't help that he entered her dreams…sequences that switched from happy to sad without rhyme or reason.

Consequently she woke feeling as if she hadn't slept at all. Worse, her head threatened a doozy of a headache, and she'd have given almost anything to be able to take the day off.

Except it wasn't an option. She had work to do, things to organise…

Rise and shine, she bade herself silently as she slid from the bed. Time to shower, dress, eat breakfast, grab a caffeine fix, then *move it.*

CHAPTER THREE

ONE day bled into another: hectic long hours where multi-tasking became a necessity, not an option, and sleep was something Gianna sought in the late-night hours, only to wake at dawn and repeat the process all over again.

Somewhere in there she factored in a call to Ben, explained her decision, and listened to his voiced caution.

It didn't help that he disapproved...for good reason. He didn't want to see her hurt again.

'Two weeks, Ben,' she reassured him. 'I'll be with Teresa in Mallorca. Raúl will remain in Madrid most of the time.'

'I hope so, for your sake. You're determined to do this?'

'Yes. For Teresa.'

'OK, but take care,' he warned. 'And stay in touch.'

'I will.' A promise she'd keep, without fail.

Annaliese accepted the managerial position with remarkable ease, and together they conducted the interviewing, trial and selection of a new team member for Bellissima, choosing a capable salesperson with an impressive CV and a pleasant personality. Gianna elected to retain another applicant on call, should the need arise for back-up.

By week's end most everything was in place, and when the weekend—the boutique's busiest days—passed without a hitch, there seemed no logical reason not to contact Raúl.

There were, of course, any number of the *illogical* kind…most of which she'd considered and discarded several times in any one day.

Except she'd given her word and, failing an accident or illness, in a matter of days she'd board a private jet *en route* to Madrid, with Raúl in attendance.

Something she'd give almost anything to avoid.

Oh…*suck it up*, she chastised herself in silent admonition.

He was CEO of the Velez-Saldaña conglomerate. A man who worked long hours and travelled extensively.

Two weeks. Why, she'd probably only see him a few times, and then she could excuse herself on the pretext of giving mother and son quality time.

Raúl had only phoned *once* since the evening they'd shared dinner. And then the conversation had been a brief, matter-of-fact request for an update with a view to fixing a departure time.

So she made the call, and ignored the faint shivery sensation that slithered down her spine at the sound of his deep faintly accented drawl.

'Gianna.'

Why should she be surprised he had her number listed on his caller ID register? Except it was recorded as a private listing, and only essential business colleagues and close friends had been given it.

For a moment she felt inclined to pull him up on it— except he had sources, influence and possessed the manipulative power to acquire almost any information he wanted.

Cool? She could do *cool*. 'I can be available to leave Wednesday.'

'I'll have a car waiting outside your apartment complex at six Wednesday morning.'

Her back stiffened. 'I'd prefer to take a taxi and meet you at the airport.'

'Your bid for independence is admirable. Although totally unnecessary. given we'll both be heading in the same direction.' He paused imperceptibly. '*Six*, Gianna.'

She heard the faint click as he ended the call, and she tamped down the faint growl threatening to emerge from her throat.

'Problems?'

She schooled her expression at the sound of Annaliese's voice and summoned a faint smile. 'No.'

None that she couldn't deal with, she assured herself silently as she prepared to leave the boutique at midday on Tuesday. She needed to collect Jazz and deliver him to the boarding cattery, alert Reception she'd be absent from her apartment for two weeks, then pack.

At some stage she also needed to eat. And clear her refrigerator of any food liable to expire before her return.

Just do it.

Don't allow yourself to *think*.

It was late when she finally made it to bed, and she set the alarm, then prepared to sleep…only to toss and turn and wake at dawn, aware that the last thing she remembered was the digital clock read-out signalling 2:15 a.m. in luminous green.

The urge to bury her head beneath the pillow was difficult to ignore. Although the risk of sleeping through the alarm proved a sufficient deterrent, and she determinedly threw back the bedcovers.

Coffee, hot, strong and sweet, then she'd shower, do a final check of the apartment, her travel documents, dress…

It was almost six when Gianna took the elevator down to Reception, and it came as no surprise to see Raúl's tall figure positioned in the adjoining lounge area.

For a few timeless seconds his eyes locked with hers, and she determinedly ignored the slow curl of nerves set on causing havoc deep within, even while she silently damned them to hell.

His sexual alchemy proved a powerful force—something of which he was surely aware. How could he not be? she thought cynically. Women of all ages vied for his attention…openly flirting while issuing silent and not so silent invitations in a bid to discover for themselves if his reputation between the sheets held true.

To Gianna's knowledge he never took up with any of them. Except how could she know for sure?

Absent this morning was the corporate business suit, buttoned shirt and tie. Instead he'd chosen casual attire—tailored black trousers, black butter-soft leather jacket, and a white chambray shirt unbuttoned at the neck.

An overall look which emphasised his blatant masculinity and gave Gianna pause to question her sanity.

Two weeks, she reminded herself stoically. Fourteen days…most of which would pass without her seeing him at all.

So what is the problem? Begin as you mean to go on, she cautioned herself staunchly as he crossed to her side.

'Good morning.' Her voice sounded matter-of-fact, and for a second she thought she caught a glimpse of wry humour in his dark eyes before he returned the greeting.

'Ready?'

As she'd ever be, she assured herself silently as she deliberately summoned a slight smile. 'Yes.'

Except she wasn't quick enough to release her bag as Raúl reached for it, and something deep inside her quivered as his fingers came into brief contact with her own before she snatched her hand away.

So much for remaining cool, calm and collected. They hadn't even reached the airport, let alone left Australia, and already she was *twitchy.*

Oh, *great.* She had to get through a long flight before she'd be free of him. *Hours....* Too many of them, she perceived as she preceded him out to the car.

Was he aware how *unsettled* he made her feel?

For sure, Gianna conceded wryly as she slid into the passenger seat while he stowed her bag in the boot.

What did one discover as a suitable topic of conversation with an ex-lover who also happened to be her husband? Soon to be *ex*, she amended, for the path to divorce was merely a formality.

The weather? The state of world affairs? She pondered as Raúl took the ocean-front route to the airport.

What would his reaction be if she aimed straight for the jugular and queried him sweetly about his ex-lover, the self-possessed Sierra Montefiore, who'd sensed a slender crack in Gianna's marriage and closed in for the kill?

Not a good way to begin the day, the flight, or a two-week sojourn in Mallorca. So sticking to the prosaic seemed safe, not to mention wise.

Pretend, Gianna bade silently. And she did...with polite charm and considerable poise. She even played Gold Coast host by pointing out new high-rise apartment buildings, and proposed ventures in the pipeline for the rapidly growing tourist city.

Conversation carried them the thirty-minute drive to the airport, where, given Raúl's private Lear jet, passage through Customs proved a mere formality before they were cleared to board.

There were introductions to the pilot and flight staff,

whereupon Raúl discarded his jacket, turned back his sleeve-cuffs, they took their seats and all too quickly were in the air.

Gianna reached down into her carry-on bag and extracted a thick new release by a favourite author, and spared Raúl a glance.

'Please don't feel you need to entertain me.' She even managed a faint smile. 'I'll be perfectly happy reading.'

'Breakfast will be served in about an hour.' Was that her imagination, or did the edge of his mouth twitch in amusement? 'You have no objection if I work?'

She met his dark eyes with equanimity. 'Not at all.'

Raúl inclined his head, extracted a laptop, and set to work, wrapping up configurations on screen, then transferring data from various files to update various graphs.

The ability to achieve total focus had been something he'd acquired during university studies. That and a photographic mind had ensured a smooth passage as he earned one degree after another, choosing employment for three years in New York before returning to Madrid to join his father in the Velez-Saldaña conglomerate.

On his father's demise Raúl had assumed the position of CEO and developed the firm into a worldwide conglomerate, accumulating a personal fortune which included prime real estate in several cities around the world, industrial holdings—you name it.

He had it all…amend that to *nearly* all. One thing was missing. Perhaps the most important, he mused. The love of a good woman…*family*.

Not *any* woman. Gianna…who had been *his*, until life had thrown a curve ball and she had walked.

Divorce hadn't been on his agenda. Nor hers, apparently. *Yet*.

Circumstance had presented him with a two-week

window in which to ensure she would never consider it an option.

Flight staff served a full breakfast an hour later, from which Gianna selected muesli, fruit and coffee.

Given the time zone, she calculated they were due to arrive in Madrid late Tuesday, thereby gaining almost a full day.

'Won't it be an imposition to arrive at Teresa's villa at such a late hour?' The query held no validity, for, although the villa was fully staffed, Raúl would naturally possess the relevant keys to gain access.

He regarded her thoughtfully as he reached for his coffee. He drained his cup and refilled it from the carafe. 'We'll stay overnight at my apartment, then fly to Mallorca tomorrow morning.'

His apartment? *Not in this millennium.*

Her eyes sparked brilliant blue fire. 'I'll book into a hotel.'

'Afraid, Gianna?'

'Of you? *No.*'

'In which case you have no reason for concern,' he drawled in response.

Sure, she decided silently. *And pigs might fly.*

It was relatively simple to pretend an intense interest in the book she was reading—except in truth she barely retained a paragraph or two on each page she turned. The plot was predictable, but she was a fan of the author's style and individual voice.

Raúl's presence provided a distraction, one she found impossible to ignore, and after a while she simply secured a marker, closed the book, then, feeling strangely restless, stood to her feet and stretched her legs by covering the length of the jet several times.

He, on the other hand, didn't appear a *wit* disturbed as

he worked throughout the flight, logging in the hours as if it was a normal day at the office...his focus total.

Did he even notice she was *there*?

Somehow it annoyed her, the fact that he might not—which hardly made any sense. *What was wrong with her?*

Something she silently questioned as the hours wound down to arrival time, and the nerves in her stomach began tightening into a painful ball as the jet began to lose altitude in preparation for landing.

There was something vaguely surreal about disembarking in the night hours after a long flight, and seeing Raúl's driver, Carlos, move forward to meet them as they entered the arrivals lounge.

Within a matter of minutes they were comfortably seated in Raúl's luxury Mercedes, their luggage stowed in the boot, and the car eased towards an exit.

Gianna leaned forward a little. 'Could you please check hotel accommodation and book a room for me, Carlos?'

She glimpsed the driver's questioning look via the rear vision mirror. *'Señor?'*

'The apartment,' Raúl countered smoothly.

She threw him a dark glare, which lost much of its impact in the shadowy interior. 'I'd prefer a hotel,' she reiterated with quiet vehemence.

Only to have him remind her, 'There are three guest suites.'

As if she didn't know this. She'd *lived* there with him for a time.

The rational part of her brain registered that it was late at night, it had been a long day, and all she wanted to do was shower, then climb into bed and sleep.

What difference did it make *where*?

Except for the niggle of resentment at his intent to take control.

His eyes locked with her own. 'Give it up, Gianna.' His voice was deceptively quiet, and her eyes sparked retaliatory anger for a few long seconds before she deliberately turned her attention to the passing nightscape as Carlos joined the main arterial route into the city.

The thought of revisiting the penthouse apartment she'd shared with Raúl in the exclusive area of Salamanca meant a revival of memories she'd chosen to mentally compartmentalise in a box labeled *'Past,'* where they lay buried in the deep recesses of her mind. Never to be retrieved, opened and re-examined…except in the intrusive dreams she was unable to control.

When she had left Madrid, she'd only taken what she had brought into the relationship. All the gifts he'd generously bestowed…clothing, lingerie, jewellery…had been left behind.

Had he changed anything? Redecorated? Removed all traces of her occupation?

Oh, get over yourself, Gianna silently chided. Why balk at *one night* in a luxury two-level penthouse apartment? Raúl's master suite and his home office occupied the upper level. The guest suites, lounge, dining room and service rooms were situated on the lower level.

Why, she'd probably only see him in the morning, when Carlos drove them to the airport.

So what was the big deal?

There was none…except in her mind.

Consequently she exited the Mercedes as it drew to a halt in the forecourt, rode a lift to the apartment, allowed Raúl to deposit her bag in one of the guest suites, then politely bade him goodnight.

Unpack, shower, then bed, she determined, and completed each before sliding beneath the covers.

Yet sleep eluded her, and she tossed and turned, caught up in a number of complex reactions. Vivid memories of happier times, the starkness of their break-up…and inevitably wondering if she'd made the right decision in coming here.

Teresa—think only of Teresa.

Except nothing eased the haunting pain, until with a low growl of anguish she slid from the bed and moved quietly into the kitchen.

Hot milk with a dash of brandy might soothe her jangling nerves, overcome the jetlag and tension and allow her a few hours' rest.

Easy to fill a beaker with milk from the refrigerator and heat it in the microwave. When it was done she added a generous nip of brandy, hesitated, added another, then cupped her hands around the beaker and crossed to the window to look out at the nightscape, where pinpricks of light illuminated tall buildings and bright neon advertisements blazed in cascading colour.

Raúl stirred at the faint beeping sound of the security monitor, saw the flashing sensor light position the lounge, and moved quietly from the bed, taking only a brief moment to pull on jeans before descending the stairs to investigate.

Had the main entrance been breached, several security measures would have been automatically activated and a security team would already be on their way.

As it was internal there was only one logical explanation…Gianna.

He entered the lounge and saw her standing before the floor-to-ceiling plate glass.

Her slender form silhouetted there aroused a tug of emotion he tamped down.

She was attired in cotton sleep trousers and tank top, hair pulled into a loose ponytail, and her features appeared pale beneath the dimmed lighting.

'Unable to sleep?'

The sound of his voice startled her, and she turned, eyes widening as he crossed to stand at her side.

He had the soft tread of a cat, and she instinctively hugged her arms across her midriff.

'Several hours of air travel, I guess,' she managed evenly.

'You didn't sleep during the flight.'

How did he know that she'd simply closed her eyes and pretended sleep because she was unable to relax sufficiently in his presence? She hadn't expected to feel vulnerable, or so acutely sensitive…and it made her cross.

Oh, for heaven's sake, call it like it is… She was edgy, uncertain in hindsight if she'd made the right decision to place herself in a position where she'd be constantly reminded of what had been, not to mention the fallout of leaving Spain, leaving *Raúl*. Revisiting it again now seemed to be the height of foolishness.

Yet she was here, and after breakfast the Velez-Saldaña private jet would transport her to Mallorca, where Teresa's villa in Cala Fornells, Calvià, would provide panoramic views of the sea and an escape from Raúl's disturbing presence.

None of which helped *now*, as he stood close, within touching distance, his tall, partly clothed frame a vivid reminder of times past when she'd slipped from their bed unable to sleep. Occasions when he'd gently massaged her neck, shoulders, easing the kinks, before sweeping her into his arms and carrying her back to bed.

For one brief moment she almost longed for the soporific effect…the comfort. She was aware the sensual tension still existed on her part. But on his?

He was impossible to read, and she tried to convince herself she didn't *want* to.

Worse, to stand here, *aware* and almost compliant, was the antithesis of the image she cared to present. *Dammit*, she could sense the clean male scent of him, the faint muskiness merging with his brand of aftershave.

It evoked too many memories…places she was loath to go.

With determined effort, she drank the rest of her milk, then indicated the empty beaker. 'I'll take this through to the kitchen, then go back to bed.' She waited a beat, then added, 'Goodnight…' with the utmost politeness.

He made no attempt to stop her, and there was a small part of her that almost wished he would.

Are you insane?

The words echoed silently as she slid into bed and snapped off the bed-lamp, becoming the last thing she remembered before she fell asleep.

CHAPTER FOUR

A NOTE propped within easy visibility rested on the counter when Gianna entered the kitchen.

> I've eaten. Help yourself. The jet leaves at nine for Mallorca. R

There was a sense of relief in eating alone, and she selected cereal, fruit, and strong sweet black coffee, then checked the newspaper headlines, surprised at how easily she recalled her fluency with the Spanish language.

Soon Carlos would drive her to the airport where she'd board the Velez-Saldaña jet for Mallorca. Where at least she'd be free from Raúl's presence.

Sure, he'd fly in on occasion to visit with Teresa…but not every day.

Short social visits she could cope with, she rationalised a few minutes before nine, as she transferred toiletries into her bag, closed the zip and emerged into the lounge.

Raúl was already there, conducting a conversation in French on his cellphone. Not exactly a surprise—*business* encompassed a large part of his life.

Unless he was touching base with a woman…the mere thought of which sent unexpected pain lancing through her body.

She shifted her gaze and felt her heart jolt at the sight of a large overnight bag resting on the floor at his feet.

Please tell me he doesn't intend to visit Mallorca.

Although why shouldn't he? Teresa was his mother, and he'd been absent in Australia for a week.

At that moment he cut the call and turned towards her.

'Good morning. Ready?'

'Hi,' she said evenly, and indicated her bag. 'Yes.'

'Let's go.' He collected both bags and together they exited the apartment, took the lift down to ground level, where Carlos waited ready to drive them to the airport.

The flight to Mallorca was uneventful, their arrival low-key, with a car and driver waiting to transport them to Teresa's luxury villa in Calvià.

There was something magical about the Balearic Islands…especially Mallorca, Gianna reflected, with its mansions and villas, the lush green hills and the sparkling waters. It was a true panoramic vista that always stirred Gianna's senses…offering tranquillity and a slower pace than Madrid.

Teresa's villa was situated on elevated landscaped land with carefully tended gardens, whose multi-coloured flora were scrupulously maintained. High ornate gates guarded entrance to a semi-circular driveway which led to a beautiful two-level home whose massive double wooden bronze-studded doors were open in welcome.

It was there Teresa greeted them—a slender woman of average height in her early sixties, who hugged Gianna close with obvious affection before she turned to her son and embraced him as he lowered his head, touching his lips first to one cheek, then the other.

'You brought her to me,' Teresa said softly. 'Thank you.'

Raúl held Teresa close, then gently brushed his lips to her forehead in a gesture that tore at Gianna's heartstrings.

'Yes,' he responded softly. 'Anything you ask of me.'

Which begged the question—*had he been reluctant to comply with Teresa's wishes*? And, if so, *why*? Because he'd moved on? Was Raúl contemplating divorce proceedings, too, as *she* already had?

And *why* did that possibility suddenly cause a shaft of pain? It hardly made sense. But then what did in the current scenario...except a mutual love and affection for Teresa?

The *only* reason Gianna had agreed to travel to Mallorca.

'I've had Elena prepare two suites in the guest wing,' Teresa began. 'Raúl, feel free to make use of the home office while you're here.'

Raúl was *staying?* Dear heaven...for *how long*?

Not...*please*...for the entire two weeks, surely? He had a huge conglomerate to oversee. Yet with modern technology he could do that from almost anywhere in the world.

A fact which irked her unbearably, and she barely veiled the gleam of anger threatening to appear in her vivid blue eyes.

A faint smile teased the edges of his mouth, almost as if he could read the passage of her thoughts.

'Go freshen up—change if you wish,' Teresa offered. 'Then join me for coffee on the terrace. It's very peaceful there at this time of day.'

Sadly, Gianna noticed, Teresa's slender frame had diminished a little, and the beautiful dark eyes appeared to have lost some of their sparkle.

Gianna's heart ached, and she fought to keep the unbidden well of tears at bay as she turned towards the staircase.

The villa was well planned, its physical structure comprising a large central area containing a spacious marble-tiled entry foyer, high ceilings and a wide sweeping stair-case curving to the upper level, dividing the villa into two wings. One of them was devoted to Teresa's private rooms, while the opposite housed four guest suites. At ground level a large formal lounge and dining room, media and entertainment rooms fanned to the right of the entry foyer, with library, home office and informal lounge and dining room housed to the left. A spacious kitchen, utility rooms and staff quarters were contained in an adjoining building and connected to the villa by an enclosed walkway.

Teresa loved to entertain, Gianna reflected as she ascended the magnificent staircase, and was a dedicated fundraiser for children's charities. Her Madrid mansion had often been thrown open to host a variety of functions.

Mallorca was Teresa's sanctuary, providing a low-key lifestyle where she retreated to relax and unwind. Now she'd made it her permanent home.

'Choose, Gianna.'

The sound of Raúl's drawl brought her back to the present, and she lifted a hand in a non-committal gesture. 'Any one will be fine.'

'As long as it's not mine?'

She spared him a dark look. 'That doesn't even qualify for an answer.' With that, she moved past him and entered the suite at the end of the hallway. Only to discover he'd followed in her wake. 'What do you think you're doing?'

One eyebrow slanted with musing cynicism as he deposited her bag at the end of the large bed. 'I imagine you'll want to unpack.'

Gianna schooled her voice to be cool, polite. 'Thank you.'

He inclined his head, and she was willing to swear she

glimpsed amusement in those dark eyes an instant before he turned and left the suite.

Day one, she accorded wryly. Thirteen more to go. Please God, he wouldn't stay for all those remaining.

Each of the guest suites was spacious and lavishly decorated, with handcrafted furniture, walk-in wardrobes, and an adjoining *en suite* bathroom. The floor-to-ceiling windows offered a panoramic view over lush manicured lawns and gardens to the ocean.

Beautiful, she complimented silently. Tranquil, she added. It came as no surprise Teresa had chosen to spend time here, for a sense of peace permeated the air.

A double knock on the door provided a timely interruption, and when she opened it, Raúl was standing in the aperture.

'If you're ready, we'll go down together.'

To refuse would be churlish, not to mention impolite. Yet she had this innate desire to contest his every word and action. Which amounted to being *childish*, she castigated herself silently.

She was a woman of the world—confident, savvy and no longer blinded by her emotions.

'Why not?' She even managed a slight smile, something which brought a gleam of amusement to his eyes before he successfully masked it.

Chilled fresh fruit juice, aromatic black coffee, iced water and bite-size pastries were laid out on the table when they crossed through open glass doors to the terrace where Teresa was already seated.

'Ah, there you are.' The warm greeting held affection as Teresa indicated the table. 'Come, sit down and help yourselves.'

There was a tendency to say *You look well*…except that wasn't entirely true, Gianna acknowledged. Nor did it seem appropriate to offer *How do you feel?* Instead she said gently, 'It's lovely to be here with you.'

Teresa smiled, and her features came alive. 'My dear, the pleasure is all mine.'

It was impossible not to be affected by Raúl's presence, for no matter how hard she tried he was *there*…a disturbing entity which caused her heartbeat to quicken and put her on edge.

Did he know? Possibly. Although she fervently hoped not.

'Tomorrow I thought we might relax and catch up in person,' Teresa ventured. 'And my dear friend Adriana has issued an invitation for us to join her and a few close friends for lunch later in the week.'

'Whatever pleases you—providing you don't become overtired,' Raúl cautioned.

'Please, I'd be much happier simply spending time here with you,' Gianna added quickly.

Teresa merely smiled. 'And so you shall. But occasionally we will venture out a little. A change of pace, to share time with friends.' She caught her son's hooded gaze. 'You have my word I will rest for a few hours each afternoon.'

'We shall personally see that you do.'

We… What did he think he was doing, coupling them together? *Another* thing to add to the growing list of issues she intended to take up with him when they were alone.

Lunch was a convivial meal Elena prepared for them, followed by the siesta. Time which Gianna used to access her laptop, e-mail Ben, Annaliese and update her father as to her whereabouts.

It was after dinner, when Teresa had retired for the evening, that Gianna questioned Elena as to where she might find Raúl.

'The *señor* is in the office.'

Perfect. It took her only minutes to reach it, and she knocked once as a courtesy before entering the spacious room.

Raúl glanced up, inclined his head, indicated a chair, then continued talking on his cellphone as he keyed data into a laptop.

It was a terse conversation in Spanish, most of which she understood. Not entirely pleasant, she perceived as he cut the connection and met her gaze with unwavering attention.

'You have something on your mind?'

'Yes,' Gianna acknowledged succinctly, and glimpsed his wry smile as he eased back in his office chair and folded his hands behind his head.

'Which you intend to spell out in detail?'

'Put money on it.'

His slightly arched eyebrow had her launching into speech.

'What's with coupling my name with yours?' Her eyes flashed blue fire. 'There is no *we*.'

'You have a problem agreeing Teresa should conserve her energy and rest?'

'Of course not.'

'Therefore your objection is…?'

She wanted to throw something at him, and she briefly weighed up a few possible items on the desk, caught the way his eyes darkened in silent warning…and refused to be intimidated.

'Dammit, I don't need you to speak on my behalf.'

His eyes seared her own, watchful, assessing. 'It bothers you that Teresa requested I join her in spending time with you?'

Teresa had? 'You could have told me.'

His eyes didn't move from her own. 'To what purpose?'

Because I could have prepared myself.

How *stupid* was that?

Nothing she did would have made a difference…not before or *now*.

Raúl was a force unto himself, with the power to damage her emotional heart. And she hated him for it. What was worse, she hated *herself* for being so foolishly vulnerable.

'Just know I'm not happy about it,' she said at last. 'The less time we spend in each other's company, the better.'

He inclined his head. 'Anything else?'

Whatever made her think she could verbally best him?

'Not at the moment.'

'Are you sure about that, *querida*?' he taunted softly, and watched faint pink colour her cheeks as she looked at him in stark disbelief.

'If you think…' Words temporarily failed her. 'Are you mad?'

Yet the thought of his mouth on her own…his hands shaping her body… *Oh, God, she had to get out of here.*

'Go to hell.' She hated that her voice sounded shaky as she turned and walked from the room.

Damn him. The curse pounded silently in her mind as she crossed the hallway and entered her suite. She was so impossibly *angry*…with him, herself.

The temptation to pack a bag, call a taxi and take the first flight to Madrid, then *home* was almost impossible to ignore.

Yet how could she leave when she'd committed to spend time with Teresa? The analogy *caught between a rock and a hard place* seemed incredibly apt.

So *simmer down*—do a few calisthenics to work off the anger, shower, then retire to bed with a book.

It was a feasible plan and she went through the motions, donned sleep trousers, tank top, and slid into bed to read until the words blurred.

CHAPTER FIVE

IT WAS a beautiful morning, Gianna noted as she checked the scene from her bedroom window. Lush green lawns provided a lovely background to the meticulously shaped shrubs which stood like miniature rounded sentinels in perfect symmetry.

She opened the window and heard soft cascading water from the fountain, felt the slight breeze whispering in from the sea with its faint salty tang.

Heaven.

Almost, she qualified, if it wasn't for Raúl's presence at the villa. He bothered her in a way she was loath to examine in any depth.

From a distance of several thousand kilometres, on the other side of the world, she'd been able to convince herself she was over him and had moved on.

Up close and personal, such convictions were proved totally erroneous. Something that was becoming more glaringly apparent with every passing day...and there were still *twelve* to go.

Teresa and Raúl were already seated out on the terrace when Gianna joined them, and although Teresa's smile was bright she looked tired and quite pale.

Not such a good day, Gianna surmised as she leant forward to bestow a light kiss to the older woman's cheek.

'Coffee?' It was Raúl who posed the query, and who moved to fill her cup with the steaming aromatic brew.

His close presence stirred her senses, and for an instant she was transported back to a time when it had seemed a natural gesture to lift her face to receive the teasing brush of his lips on her own, the intimate smile in acknowledgement of the night spent in each other's arms…her body still vibrantly alive from his possession.

Now there was only politeness, as a courtesy to Teresa's presence. And Gianna had no sensible reason for wishing it to be otherwise…only knew that there was a kernel of sadness deep inside she was unable to dispense.

Crazy, she acknowledged silently, as she added sugar and sipped the delicious coffee.

'I trust you slept well?'

'Fine, thank you,' she responded with a smile, and crossed her fingers beneath the table to excuse the fabrication.

'I have broached tonight's scheduled charity function with Raúl,' Teresa began. 'Its purpose is to raise funds for terminally ill children. It's a cause close to my heart, and one my late husband and I founded early in our marriage. Unfortunately I'm not feeling up to an evening out.'

Gianna felt the nerves in her stomach stir as Teresa turned towards her, and uttered a silent prayer…only to have it unanswered.

'I would consider it a favour to me if you'd agree to act as Raúl's partner for the evening.'

To refuse would not only be churlish, but unkind, so she didn't even consider it, merely qualifying, 'It will be a pleasure, unless Raúl has any objection.' Such as another woman waiting in the wings… Sierra, or his current lover.

'Why would I object?' Raúl queried with an indolent drawl, and Teresa's face brightened with delight.

'Thank you.' She named a luxury hotel in Palma, then turned towards Gianna and offered a conspiratorial smile. 'It'll provide an opportunity for you to go shopping.'

Gianna did a quick mental search of the clothes she'd brought with her…and failed to come up with anything suitable to wear.

'We'll drive into Palma after breakfast,' Raúl stated.

We will?

'I can easily take a taxi,' she offered sweetly.

'My dear,' Teresa intervened gently, 'Raúl would never permit it.'

The steady look he cast Gianna challenged her to argue. 'We'll aim to leave at nine.'

And that, it appeared, put an end to the subject…at least in Teresa's presence. But not, Gianna determined, until the moment she'd inform him she intended to conduct her shopping expedition *solo*.

Something which occurred in the hallway of their shared guest wing as she prepared to leave a written note to that effect in his office.

'Hoping to get away undetected?'

It seemed as if he'd appeared out of nowhere. How did he *do* that?

She tilted her chin, and her eyes sparked dark chips. 'There's absolutely no need for you to accompany me.'

'I disagree.' His drawl held a tinge of wry amusement.

'Please don't give me any of that *macho* hyperbole about a woman alone.'

One eyebrow arched in silent query. 'You *want* to be prey to skilled pickpockets? Suffer the indignity of having your wallet filched beneath the guile of a supposedly accidental jolt while you're momentarily distracted? Find your cellphone has somehow disappeared, and you need to find a police station in order to call the villa for help?'

'And you're prepared to *save* me from any of this by walking at my side? *Really? You,* of course, are exempt from any nefarious miscreants?'

'Yes.'

'*Naturally,*' she concurred sweetly. 'One look from you, and any mis-intentioned pickpocket will run in the opposite direction.'

'You doubt it?'

No. But she wouldn't own to it for all the tea in China. Instead she directed him a dark glare, then turned and moved swiftly towards the head of the staircase…only to discover he'd deliberately kept pace with her.

'I'll call a taxi.' It was a last-ditch effort for independence, which merely incurred a swift brooding look more effective than any words could be.

'You really are the most annoying, incredibly arrogant man I've ever had the misfortune to meet,' Gianna flung at him when they reached the spacious garage, and she stood in defiant silence as he used a remote to unlock the · Mercedes.

'Get in, Gianna.'

His voice was dangerously quiet, and there was something apparent in his dark eyes that warned retribution if she chose to argue further.

In the name of heaven, *why* was she behaving like a recalcitrant child? She had never thrown a tantrum in her life, or given in to a hissy fit…even in the most dire of circumstances.

So why *now*?

Because every moment she spent in Raúl's presence highlighted what they'd both shared, and her anger was merely a mechanism to shore up the protective barriers she'd erected against him.

Because she was desperately afraid he might break those barriers down...and, worse, dispense with them.

And then where would she be?

Right back where she'd been three years ago...a heart-broken mess.

A bitter laugh rose and died in her throat.

Self-preservation.

OK, so she'd do this.

Without a further word she slid into the front passenger seat, fastened the seat belt, and sat in silence as Raúl sent the powerful car out through the gates.

Where were they heading? El Corte Inglés at the Avenidas in Palma? Or would he seek a boutique in any one of several luxury hotels?

A hotel boutique, she determined as he sought valet parking, then ushered her into a boutique where the *vendeuse* greeted him by name and almost genuflected with enthusiasm at a promised sale.

Raúl Velez-Saldaña happened to be a well-known identity whose photograph often graced the media. Recognition didn't necessarily mean he'd purchased gowns or high-end designer shoes here for other women.

And why should it concern her if he had?

Because it does... Which hardly made any sense. She no longer loved him. Hell, she didn't even *like* him.

Liar.

Why else had she become a restless sleeper, knowing he slept in a suite only metres from her own?

Each time she saw him, she was conscious of an elevated nervous tension. He had only to touch her and her heart pulsed to a faster beat.

What was that if it wasn't the existence of sensual awareness?

The sane, sensible part of her warned that she didn't need it...most certainly didn't want it in her life. Not with *him*...not with any man.

No longer would she toy with the idea of divorce. As soon as she returned to Australia she'd consult her lawyer and have him file the necessary papers.

'This one, I think.'

The sound of Raúl's voice followed by the *vendeuse*'s concurring approval caught Gianna's attention, and her eyes widened at the sight of a deep sapphire-blue exquisitely cut gown in silk chiffon with a ruched bodice, slender spaghetti straps, and a slender layered skirt.

As much as she hated to admit it...it was perfect.

'Fortunately it's the young lady's size.'

'My wife,' Raúl corrected with calm indolence, and Gianna's mouth opened to deny it, only to have him press light fingers to her lips. 'You can thank me later, *querida*.'

Darling? Lover? Whatever interpretation you chose to apply, neither held true...at least not anymore.

She was so tempted to bite him, it almost *hurt* to resist. And he *knew*.

'Shoes,' he said calmly. 'And an evening purse.'

If she could, she'd tell him exactly what he could do with both items. The only thing that stopped her was an adherence to polite good manners.

Yet when she stepped into the gown, slid her feet into the stiletto heeled evening sandals and checked the mirrored effect, she had to concede both Raúl and the *vendeuse* had nailed it.

There was no way she could top it, and her pleased smile said it all. 'Thank you.'

'Your husband has a good eye,' the *vendeuse* complimented as she clapped her hands and tilted her head to one side. 'Your hair, *señora*… Might I suggest you style it up? You have such a slender neck it is a pity not to display it. Diamond ear-studs,' she enthused. 'A slim matching bracelet and perhaps a diamond pendant. Not too much to take away from the gown, *comprende*?' She moved to stand behind Gianna and freed the zip fastening. 'I will package the items while you change, *sí*?'

It took only minutes to pull on tailored trousers, add her blouse, then slip her feet into her footwear.

She emerged from the fitting room to discover Raúl in the process of using his credit card, and she crossed quickly to the sales counter.

'I'll pay for the purchases.'

The *vendeuse* paused and cast him an enquiring glance. *'Señor?'*

'My wife's independence is laudable,' he opined smoothly. 'However, in this instance you will disregard it.'

'As you wish.'

'I would prefer…' Gianna faltered as Raúl cupped her face and covered her mouth with his own in a soft kiss that tore the breath from her throat.

'No.' A gentle remonstrance, but effective, and her eyes widened at the sensual gleam apparent in those dark eyes as he released her.

The atmosphere between them suddenly became highly charged, and for several heart-stopping seconds she was oblivious to everything in the room as she stood in a state of mesmerised inaction.

'Your packages, *señor*.'

The sound of the *vendeuse*'s voice acted as a catalyst

that brought her back to reality, and she shook her head in a gesture that indicated acquiescence. 'Men,' she confided with a faintly wry smile. 'Generous to a fault.'

'Ah, but *señora*,' the vendeuse chided gently. 'What woman would not value such a man?'

Gianna merely offered a winsome smile, and waited until they exited the boutique and were out of earshot before venting quietly, 'What on earth were you *thinking*?'

'To what do you refer?'

'Don't toy with me. You know perfectly well what I mean.'

'You are angry because I bought you a gown?'

She shot him a baleful glare. 'Try again.'

'You object because I kissed you?'

'That,' she allowed through gritted teeth, 'and referring to me as your *wife*.'

'*Querida*,' he reminded her gently. 'You *are* my wife.'

Not for much longer. Words she almost said aloud... only for them to remain unuttered, and for the life of her she failed to understand *why*.

'Shall we share coffee?' Raúl suggested, indicating the hotel lounge. 'Practice,' he drawled with a touch of indolent humour, 'for the evening ahead.'

Fun. But not the kind she looked forward to experiencing.

Yet you've been there before, remember? The social occasions, some of which had required attendance by the wealthy elite, and she'd excelled first as Raúl's partner, then as his wife.

A strange ache settled deep in her heart and became a tangible pain. They'd been so happy, so very much in tune...until it all went wrong.

Enough. She'd replayed that fateful scene so many times

she could repeat verbatim every word Sierra had uttered. It was like a bad movie played by hostile characters with no happy resolution.

Now there was only the road ahead…one she'd successfully forged on her own. Surely she could survive a two-week sojourn *sans* any emotional damage?

Consequently she chose a comfortable hotel lounge chair, sank back into it, sipped excellent coffee and attempted to fit Raúl into the mould of casual friend.

It didn't work… How on earth had she expected it to work? He'd been her lover, and just *looking* at him revived vivid memories of what they'd once shared. Almost to the point where she could *feel* his hands on her body, his mouth devouring her own, the intimacies…

Oh, dear God…*stop*.

She met his thoughtful gaze and offered a stunning smile. It was purely a defence mechanism, one she deliberately adopted in an attempt to fill the time.

Soon they'd return to the car, drive to Calvià, enjoy a light lunch, hopefully with Teresa, who acted as a perfect buffer. Given the customary siesta, after which she could plead time out to connect with her laptop, it would soon be time to shower, tend to her hair, make-up and dress.

Apropos of which, she offered Raúl a perfunctory thanks.

The gown bore an expensive price-tag, the evening sandals were designer, the evening purse… All totalled close to an amount that made her blink.

'I appreciate your assistance in purchasing the gown, the shoes. Thank you,' she said, and tried to ignore the way her heartbeat quickened at his lazy smile. 'However, I insist on reimbursing you.'

'Consider it a gift.'

* * *

He was such a strong and vital man…way too much for any one woman to handle with ease. And yet she had…for a while. Loving him with everything she had, everything she was…heart, mind, soul.

Don't go there. It served no purpose.

'*No,*' she insisted. 'I cannot possibly permit you to pay for anything on my behalf.'

He regarded her with indolent amusement. 'And why is that?'

There was never going to be a better time. 'Because I intend to file for divorce.'

She wasn't sure what she expected from him. Agreement? Expressed regret? An attempt at persuasion to change her mind?

Who could tell from his unchanged expression? The man was a skilled strategist, adept in concealing any apparent reaction.

'You don't perceive another solution?'

There was little she could do about the slow curl of her stomach. 'Such as?'

He took his time in answering. 'Reconciliation.'

Gianna looked at him in stark disbelief. 'Are you out of your mind?'

'We still share a mutual attraction. That's something to build on rather than discard, don't you think?'

Her response was instantaneous. 'No.'

How could she even begin to entertain anything like his suggestion.

Re-enter his life, his bed—dear heaven—be subjected to Sierra's machinations, and those of the various women who tried to tempt him? *No.* She couldn't…*wouldn't* do it. That path lay strewn with the kind of pain she refused to revisit.

But what of the good times? a silent voice taunted. The

loving? What they'd shared in bed and out of it? The joy, being so in tune with each other there had been no need for words? His wicked mouth…how easily he could arouse her to a depth of passion she hadn't known existed? What of that?

Oh, *please*. Sex, even *very good sex*, wasn't a basis for marriage. *So don't even go there!*

So why this secret longing in a part of her heart for what once had been? How could she revisit and recapture the past…and not deal with what had torn everything apart?

Fidelity, once breached, made it almost impossible to repair trust. All she had to do was control her emotions— and the effect they were having on her body…and her heart.

Her mind ran on. A reconciliation would mean a total change to her life as she knew it. Could she move back to Spain? Give up her business and everything she'd done to put her life back on an even kilter?

It didn't even bear consideration.

'No.' Her voice was firm in reiteration.

It was a relief when they finished their coffee and he instructed the concierge to summon the car, and she sat in silence during the drive to the villa.

There was pleasure in witnessing Teresa's delight with the contents of the various designer-emblazoned carry-bags.

'Perfect,' Teresa enthused. 'Raúl has an excellent eye. His late father possessed the same ability.'

In all aspects? Gianna queried silently. Had Sebastiano Velez-Saldaña also cheated on his wife during their marriage?

Doubtful, given the photographic images which portrayed them as a devoted and loving couple.

Yet images could be deceptive. Hadn't she proved that by posing at Raúl's side with a loving smile when inside she'd been racked with heartsick pain?

CHAPTER SIX

'NERVOUS?'

The foyer adjacent to the hotel ballroom held numerous invited guests, standing together in various groups as uniformed waiters offered a variety of drinks and canapés as they moved among the crowd.

Gianna lifted the slim flute to her lips and took a sip of champagne. 'Have I reason to be?'

Raúl's dark eyes pierced her own. 'No.'

He looked incredible, attired in an impeccably tailored black evening suit, white linen shirt and black bow-tie. Striking, she amended. His skin tone, sculpted broad bone structure highlighting a strong jawline, the generous, sensual mouth, and eyes as dark as sin.

Attractively rugged, rather than traditionally handsome. Powerful, intensely primitive. She'd seen him in action brokering a deal...and witnessed the ruthlessness apparent, his forbidding ability to cut and walk away.

Which brought the question as to why, after he'd followed her and she'd rejected him, he hadn't filed for divorce? Unless it *suited* him to appear to remain married.

For what reason? she persisted, and gave it up as being too complex to examine in any detail...at least right *now*.

'Raúl,' a deep, heavily accented voice greeted him. 'Good to see you.'

Gianna turned slightly and saw a man similar to Raúl in height and age, whose rugged features and sharply focused dark eyes categorised him as a likely business colleague.

'Rafael.' The acknowledgement emerged with a briskness that bore politeness more than friendship, and she saw Raúl's eyes harden a little as the other man switched his attention to her.

'Aren't you going to introduce me?'

She recognised the type—astute and a bit of a rake, sure of his effect on women, and content to play the seduction game.

'No.'

Rafael's eyes gleamed with wicked humour. 'Special, hmm?' He cast her a speculative look. 'I can see why.' His smile held such warmth it could have melted ice. 'At least tell me your name.'

She wanted to laugh, his approach was so brazen. 'Gianna.'

'Velez-Saldaña,' Raúl added with an edge to his voice only a fool would ignore.

'A relative?'

'My wife.'

'Ah.' Comprehension was swift and accompanied by a wry smile. 'I am not surprised you guard her so well.'

'Indeed.'

A soft laugh escaped Rafael's lips. 'My cue, I think, to move along.'

Raúl merely inclined his head, and Gianna waited a few seconds before offering a sallying reproof beneath the guise of a visibly sweet smile. 'Must you behave like a proprietorial oaf?'

For a moment she thought he might laugh, and her eyes narrowed in silent warning beneath his gleaming gaze.

'Most men are proprietorial with their women.'

'Correction…I'm no longer *your* woman.'

His gaze remained steady as he took his time to gently query, 'No?'

She could give no plausible reason why the air between them suddenly became electrically charged…nor could she explain why her pulse quickened to a drumming beat.

For a moment she almost swayed beneath a wave of raw primal heat, and she hated that he sensed it.

The hotel, the guests, even the *reason* she was there, faded beyond the periphery of her vision so there was only *him*.

He made no attempt to touch her, which was just as well, for she seemed to have temporarily lost her sense of reality, adrift in a mindless sea of remembered passion.

An intrusive sound shattered the vivid image, and she blinked as the room and its occupants swam back into focus, together with the realisation that the guests were beginning to move into the ballroom.

Staff were on hand to check tickets and offer directions to reserved tables, and it was a relief to discover she recognised two of the couples sharing their table.

Charming company, excellent food and interesting conversation made for a pleasant evening, with funds raised exceeding expectations. The entertainment provided some comedic humour, a magician and his assistant, and the usual speeches extolled the charity's achievements, goals, and made a plea for guests to donate generously.

The evening provided vivid memories of other similar functions Gianna had attended in the past, mostly at venues in Madrid with Raúl. Occasions when she'd sparkled in company, able to converse with ease, secure that the man at her side was as much hers as she was *his*.

Her presence here tonight with Raúl after such a long

absence would raise speculative interest and it bothered her that he was doing nothing to dispel it.

Playing a part, she rationalised as he leant in close to refill her glass.

Why was she so acutely attuned to him on a sexual level, when all her instincts almost screamed a warning to cut and run away from him as fast as she could before…*what*?

She succumbed and slept with him?

As if!

That wasn't going to happen…not now, not ever. For there was no way she'd venture down that road again.

Yet it was impossible not to remember how it felt to be held by him…kissed until her mind went blank…made love to as if the world would soon end.

Haunting and undeniably taunting…notching up the sensual heat several degrees as fire raced through her veins.

Hell.

With considerable effort she forced her breathing to slow to an even beat, then reached for her glass and took a measured sip of chilled wine.

Better…but not by much.

Did he sense the emotional chaos his close proximity caused her? She fervently hoped not.

A few of the guests began gathering on the dance floor as music started to play.

'Shall we join them?'

Gianna met Raúl's faintly mocking gaze and effected a slight shrug. 'Why not?'

A foolish move, she decided within minutes, as the beat changed and he drew her close…too close…and easily resisted her effort to put a little space between them.

'What do you think you're doing?'

'Dancing,' he drawled as he held her there, with one

hand resting low beneath the back of her waist in a hold that was the antithesis of conventional.

'Why not call it what it is?'

A soft, almost undetectable sound emerged from his throat. 'A reminder of how things used to be between us?'

Yes. Damn him.

A time when she'd exulted in the anticipation of how the evening would end…the subtle teasing, the warmth of his breath close to her ear as he softly relayed how they'd make love, building the sensual tension until she'd positively *ached* for them to be alone.

'If you don't want me to *accidentally* kick your ankle,' Gianna managed sweetly, 'I suggest you step back a little.'

'Fighting words, *querida*?'

It was the endearment responsible for her swift retaliatory action…and to give him credit he didn't so much as wince or miss a step.

The only warning she received was the sudden flex of his bicep beneath her hand, then his mouth covered her own in a kiss that stopped the breath in her throat.

Deliberately erotic, it invaded, branded her his own, then gentled a little before he lifted his head to regard her with dark brooding eyes.

The temptation to slap his face was almost impossible to resist, and it was only the stark realisation of time and place that cautioned against such an action.

But just wait until the moment we're alone.

'That was unforgivable.' She hated the slight quiver in her voice, and could do nothing to still the faint shivery sensation feathering down her spine.

Almost as if he knew, he slid a soothing hand in its

wake, and briefly touched his lips to her temple. 'Let's get out of here.'

They did. Raúl followed courtesy by touching base with the charity organiser, a member of the committee, then paused to bid goodnight to a few friends and business acquaintances *en route* to one of the exits.

'It's wonderful to see you both reunited,' a feminine voice offered with sincerity as they paused at a rear table.

But we're not, Gianna was inclined to inform her, and it was only the sudden tightening of Raúl's fingers in silent warning that stalled her contradiction.

He eased the vehicle into the steady stream of traffic and began heading towards Calvià.

It was a clear night, with an indigo sky in which there were the pinpricks of light from distant stars. Almost magical, if she'd been in the mood to appreciate the nightscape.

Instead she was seething from the need to keep her deep-seated anger in check...until now.

The kaleidoscope of night lights and brightly coloured neon barely registered as she visibly *killed* him with a dark look that would have quelled a lesser man.

'Just what game are you playing?' she demanded, and met his rapid glance before he returned his attention to the road ahead.

'Precisely what are you referring to?'

'All of it,' she vented, volubly incensed. 'The touchy-feely thing...*kissing* me like that.'

'Your objection being?'

'That you did it at all, *and in public*.' She paused to breathe. 'You deliberately led people to think we're...' She couldn't finish the sentence, and he did it for her.

'Together?'

'Yes. And we're not. Won't be. *Ever*,' she added for good measure.

'Then perhaps you'd care to explain the extent of your anger.'

For a moment she was speechless. 'What is this? Psychoanalysis?' Seconds later she gasped in shocked surprise as he tripped the indicator and eased the car to a halt at the kerb. 'Why are you stopping?'

Her eyes widened as he released his seat belt, then her own, and reached for her.

'Don't.' It was the one word she managed to get out before his mouth closed over hers in a gentle exploratory touch that sought to soothe her soul…then capture and reunite it with his own.

Gianna wanted to resist. And she tried, she really did, until she was swept up in the emotional tide he created and became lost—so totally lost the she was unaware of reaching up to clasp her hands together at his nape…or the fervour with which she answered his passion.

Don't think… Because if she did, she'd wrench herself from his arms and escape from the car…from *him* and the sensual magic he encapsulated without any seeming effort at all.

It was as if they had gone back in time to a place where everything was *good*. When their love had been beyond question and they'd existed solely for each other.

There were no doubts, no lack of trust…just undeniable emotion.

For a while she forgot everything…the time, the place… there was only the need for his touch as she kissed him back, exulting in the feel of him. And wanting so much more. Skin on skin…

Ohmigod… What was she *thinking*?

Correction. She wasn't thinking at all.

Reality slowly dawned, and she tore her hands from him and began using them as leverage in an effort to free herself.

At first she didn't think he'd let her go, and silent tears welled and spilled down her cheeks at the futility of the situation…worse, her reaction.

Blind lust, she attributed…almost to the point where she didn't care how or where, as long as her long-withheld desire found some form of release.

She felt like a lust-filled teenager, almost beyond control, making out in a parked car.

In a luxurious car, parked at the side of a main thoroughfare after midnight.

With Raúl.

The man to whom she was still technically married.

The man she intended to divorce.

So what the hell was she doing?

She became aware of gentle fingers brushing the tears from her cheeks, and she shook her head in distress as Raúl cradled her face.

'Don't.' It was a cry from the heart, and in one smooth movement, he released the seat back to its fullest extension, pulled her onto his lap…and simply held her.

The temptation to remain in the comfort of his arms was strong. This close, her senses were so finely attuned to him…in every way. The familiar clean male smell, the exclusive cologne he chose to wear, his strength…his gentle touch as he smoothed a few tendrils of hair that had escaped from her upswept style.

She wanted to melt into him. Yet that would never do. For how could she afford to relent when there were unresolved issues between them?

She stirred, felt his arms momentarily tighten, then at her faint protest he eased her into the passenger seat and fired the ignition.

They reached Teresa's villa in silence, and Gianna bade Raúl goodnight in the foyer, then ascended the stairs and entered her suite.

It took only minutes to undress, pull on nightwear, then she crossed to the *en suite* bathroom to unpin her hair and remove her make-up. Except the face in the mirror didn't resemble her normal reflected image. Eyes so dark and dilated; lips slightly swollen from being so thoroughly kissed.

Different.

There was no soft dreaminess apparent…just a mix of disbelief tinged with concern. She didn't want to be caught up in an emotional vortex…couldn't afford to be if she was to escape unscathed.

With every passing day she became more aware of the sensuality between them…the promise of more unless she guarded her heart—and her head.

It hurt to know how easy it would be to have sex with him. How much a part of her *craved* the intimacy. Just once. One night.

Except it wouldn't be enough…and then where would she be? Right back where she had left him three years ago. Heartbroken and bereft. Heartsick. With a need to repair the emotional damage and move on with her life…*again*.

Wasn't going to happen.

With determined effort, she applied cleanser, wiped it off, washed her face, cleaned her teeth, then studiously worked in moisturising cream before taking the pins from her hair and confining its length in a loose tail.

Go to bed and *sleep*, she bade herself silently.

It took a while to dispense with a host of haunting images, the last of which she remembered was how it felt to be held in Raúl's arms before she slid into blissful oblivion.

CHAPTER SEVEN

ANY hope Gianna held of Raúl returning to Madrid didn't appear to be fulfilled, given he chose to share breakfast with Teresa before retreating into the home office to work undisturbed until lunch.

It was on the fourth day into the first week of her two-week sojourn that Teresa announced the imminent arrival of some family members.

'They're staying with my aunt Rosita in her Palma apartment for a few days, and I've invited them to lunch today.'

Family numbered five, comprising Teresa's sister, Emilia, and her husband, Jorge, their adult children, Pablo and Cristina, and elderly Aunt Rosita. Together with Teresa and Gianna it added up to seven…*eight,* Gianna corrected as Raúl joined them.

Except his presence didn't make for *relaxed* enjoyment, and she could tell he *knew* from the faint amusement evident in his dark eyes.

Ignoring him wasn't possible, and she didn't even try.

'Teresa tells me you own a successful boutique,' Emilia began politely.

'Yes,' Gianna acknowledged with a smile. 'I stock speciality gifts. Venetian glassware, crystal, decorative bowls in various shapes and colours. Beautifully scented triple-milled soaps, exotic handmade candles...'

'Situated in a tourist holiday town, I believe?'

'It's true the Gold Coast *is* a holiday destination,' she acknowledged. 'However, it's a bustling cosmopolitan city, with a large population, multi-million-dollar homes with river and ocean frontages, beautiful beaches, shopping complexes, theme parks.'

'The climate is good?' Pablo queried. He was close to Gianna in age.

'Sub-tropical,' she relayed. 'Long summers and short mild winters.'

'You have family there?'

'My brother, Ben, and his family live in Sydney.'

'And your parents also?' Raúl's aunt questioned.

'Gianna's mother died several years ago,' Raúl informed her. 'Her father remarried and resides in Paris.'

'I see.'

No, she didn't. Who could comprehend the loss of a dearly loved mother, then too soon afterwards witnessing a father remarry and move to the other side of the world? It had felt like abandonment at the time...although with hindsight that wasn't strictly true. Their father had gifted Ben and Gianna the family home in equal shares. Ben, had already been a lawyer with excellent prospects, while she'd had steady part-time work while she studied business management.

Together they'd shared the home for three years, until Ben had married Eloise and bought out Gianna's half-share, whereupon she had purchased a flat and taken in a friend to help share expenses.

The same friend who had suggested Madrid as a holiday destination...except *holiday* had extended into a longer stay when Gianna had been offered a temporary position by one of Ben's associates based in Madrid.

It was where she had met Raúl, at an event she'd attended at the request of her employer. Glitz and glamour, Gianna recalled of the night in question, where, as corny as it sounded, she'd met Raúl's faintly hooded gaze across the crowded room and become momentarily transfixed by him, aware even then that tangling with him in any way would consign her way out of her depth, floundering in previously unchartered waters.

He'd played it cool, engaging her attention, then dazzling her with practised charm. *Putting in the groundwork,* she attributed wryly. On one level the sexual chemistry had intrigued her, and she had been tempted to explore it. Yet there had also been the intrinsic knowledge that if she did she'd become totally *lost* in the fallout.

Except her fears had been unfounded, and following a whirlwind courtship she'd agreed to move in with him.

A leap of faith, Gianna concluded, that had begun so well…

'Pablo has tickets for the opera at the Teatro Principal tonight,' Cristina ventured. 'Would you like to join us?'

'Oh, please do,' Teresa encouraged quickly. 'Raúl?'

He met Gianna's faintly desperate glance, divined it, and challenged her. 'Thank you. We'll meet you there.'

Wretch, she silently cursed him.

Teresa clapped her hands together in delight. 'It will be lovely for you to have an evening out together.'

You think?

Yet how could she deny an arrangement that appeared to give Teresa such pleasure?

'We have reservations to dine first,' Cristina added, and named a restaurant.

Oh, *joy.*

Teresa's family *had* to know of their estrangement. *Surely* an absence of three years conveyed they were living apart? On opposite sides of the world, for heaven's sake.

So why this evening's invitation? A covert attempt to bring them together?

Some chance.

Words which seemed to echo in her head as she put the final touches to her make-up, added jewellery and slid her feet into stilettos.

Formal wear meant she chose a sophisticated halter-neck gown in deep aqua silk, which flowed over her slender curves and highlighted her flawless skin. A matching silk wrap completed the outfit, and she silently thanked her instinct to pack it. She left her hair loose, collected her evening purse, crossed the suite to open the door and saw Raúl in the process of exiting his suite.

A dark evening suit shaped his form as if tailor-made for him—which it undoubtedly was.

He was something else, she admitted reluctantly as he paused, waiting for her to join him.

An intrusive presence who succeeded in putting her on edge. *In spades,* she acknowledged ruefully.

He bore a relaxed look that was deceptive, for beneath the projected persona was the mind of an intensely shrewd man who would stop at nothing to achieve his objective.

As long as it didn't include *her*, the remaining days should pass with relative pleasantness.

So why did she harbour the instinctive feeling that they were each on a different page?

Crazy, she dismissed as she walked at his side to the head of the stairs and descended them to the foyer.

'Pablo and Cristina have already left to drop their parents at Rosita's apartment,' Raúl indicated as they reached the BMW four wheel drive parked beneath the *porte-cochère.*

It was a beautiful evening, with fresh sea air drifting in from the ocean as Raúl eased the powerful vehicle toward the centre of Palma.

Traffic was beginning to build up as offices closed and staff made their way home. Soon the restaurants would begin serving those choosing to dine out, and entertainment in its various forms would attract clientele.

The hotel where Pablo had made restaurant reservations offered valet parking, and the *maître d'*'s recognition bordered on the obsequious as he escorted them to their table, personally ensuring they were comfortably seated while offering any service they required.

The power of extreme wealth and social status, Gianna acknowledged wryly.

'It would seem your reputation precedes you.'

'Specifically?'

'Why, your wit and charm, of course.'

'Of course,' Raúl mocked with a degree of amusement.

'A babe magnet,' she offered dryly. 'I can't quite pin it down to any one thing. The name Velez-Saldaña, perhaps, and all that goes with it…the villas, the apartments in various cities in the world, the luxury cars.' She tilted her head a little. 'The private jet, luxury cruiser, your—er—generous attributes.'

His eyes assumed a faintly wicked gleam. 'Would you care to elaborate on that?'

'No.'

'I've missed your refreshing honesty.'

'Oh, *please*. There were a string of women just waiting to take my place.'

'None of whom interested me.'

She looked at him carefully. 'You expect me to believe that?'

'Your prerogative.'

At that moment she saw Pablo and Cristina enter the restaurant, and after checking with the *maître d'* they made their way to the table.

Gianna liked Raúl's cousins. Pablo possessed a droll sense of humour, while Cristina *knew* fashion—what was in, what wasn't—and had the advantage of being able to determine even the most skilled copy from the genuine designer article.

'We must get together,' Cristina intimated when they'd perused the menu and placed their orders. 'I saw the most divine dress in a hotel boutique that would be perfect for you.' Her eyes sharpened a little, assessing in a way that Gianna recognised would lead to *more*. 'We'll get a manicure, have a facial, share lunch. Catch up.'

It was tempting, although her first priority had to be spending time with Teresa. Just as she was about to decline Raúl suggested, 'Why not arrange to meet in the afternoon while Teresa rests?'

'Done.' Cristina reached into her purse and extracted a pocket diary, flipped the pages and had pen poised and ready. *'When?'*

Good question. Teresa mentioned a lunch or two with friends, an evening charity event to which Velez-Saldaña leant their generous support.

'Can I get back to you on that?'

'You can.' Cristina wrote down a phone number and handed Gianna the card. 'Call me.'

Pablo offered an expressive eye-roll. 'Not to do so will be at your peril.'

'You exaggerate,' his sister rebuked.

'Do I?'

'It's called *efficiency*.'

'Officiousness.'

Cristina and Pablo shared a sibling rivalry based on teasing affection, appearing to delight in verbal sallying at every opportunity. Something, Raúl had once confided, which had existed between them since childhood.

Waitstaff presented their meal with artistic flair, and each morsel proved a delectable testament to the chef's supreme reputation.

Raúl was an urbane host, relaxed and at ease as he led Pablo into a discussion of Real Madrid's chances of winning a soccer cup final, with spirited conclusions drawn by Cristina who, Pablo teased, had her eye on one of the team players.

'Romantically,' Pablo added, only to be volubly chastised by his sister. A tirade he chose to ignore. 'They met at a party. Went on a date. He sent her flowers.'

Given Cristina made no secret of her determination to remain dedicated to her career and *single*, it was impossible not to smile, and Gianna didn't even try. 'You're not going to mention his name?'

Cristina's response was swift and fierce. 'Not if he values his life.'

A waiter's presence to take their order for coffee was timely...so, too, was the need to leave for the Teatro Principal, where a stand-out performance by a cast in splendid costume captured and held the audience's attention with breathtaking appreciation. Especially the female lead, whose clarity of voice and emotional delivery touched even the most insensitive heart.

The timed breaks between each act allowed the audience to move into the foyer, and it was there the social elite gathered and acknowledged friends.

'Raúl.'

Gianna turned slightly to see if the husky feminine purr matched the woman to whom it belonged.

It did.

Model-slim, exquisitely gowned, beautifully jewelled, with gorgeous dark hair waved in a deceptively casual style and darkly sensuous eyes with thinly veiled intent.

'Rafaela.' His acknowledgement held polite warmth, but little more.

'You should have told me you would attend the *teatro* tonight. I could have arranged for us to be seated together.'

'We're here as my cousins' guests.'

'We, *querido*?'

Oh, please, don't let's play the *invisible person* game, Gianna dismissed mentally as she proffered a polite smile.

'Gianna.'

'Another cousin, *querido*?'

'My wife.'

Rafaela's eyes flashed momentarily, although to give her credit she recovered quickly. 'The marriage is over, *sí*?'

'I have never indicated it to be.' His voice was pure silk, like the edge of a very sharp knife grazing delicate fabric, with the threat of possible damage ever present.

'But I thought...' Rafaela trailed off delicately.

'It is not something I choose to discuss.'

Gianna bore the woman's scrutiny well. She even managed a conciliatory smile as Rafaela graciously took her leave.

'One of your many conquests?'

'An acquaintance.'

'Of whom there are several.' It was a statement not a

query. 'Is that why you wear your wedding ring? To fend them off, or to provide a challenge?'

For a moment she didn't think he intended to answer, then he offered quietly, 'I haven't taken the ring off since the day you placed it there.'

She tried hard not to let his admission touch her…and failed miserably. She wanted to offer a flippant response, but somehow the words didn't find voice, and then it was too late as an announcement signified the conclusion of the intermission, and urged patrons to return to their seats.

Watching the remaining acts required concentration, something Gianna found difficult to summon, and it was something of a relief when the evening concluded.

It was only when she was alone in the car after they'd dropped Cristina and Pablo at their elderly aunt's apartment that she sought to take Raúl to task.

'Please explain why you're choosing to imply to people that our marriage is still valid.'

He spared her a dark look as the car traversed the distance to Teresa's villa. 'It isn't?'

'You know exactly what I mean.'

'It's a situation I have no inclination to change.'

But I do, she attested silently.

'Nothing to say, Gianna?' The words were a silky taunt.

'Not at this moment, no.'

They covered the remaining distance in silence, and on entering the villa, Gianna trod the staircase without offering a word until she reached the door of her suite.

'Goodnight.' Extremely polite, she pushed the door open, entered, then quietly closed the door behind her…only to sag against its rear for several long minutes before she crossed to the bed, where she dispensed with her clothes, removed her make-up and slid between the sheets.

* * *

It was a very warm day, Gianna determined as she slid out from the car and told Miguel she'd call him when she was ready for him to collect her.

The cool air-conditioned hotel lobby was pleasant as she crossed to the lounge, where Christina rose from a deep-cushioned chair to offer an effusive greeting.

Elegant in slim-line linen, stilettos, her make-up impeccable, she looked gorgeous, and Gianna offered a genuine compliment as they became seated.

'We'll order coffee,' Cristina began, 'then go shopping.'

'We don't *need* to shop.'

'Yes, we do. I've already checked out the boutique and they still have the gown in your size.'

'Give me one good reason why I need another gown?'

'Who cares about a reason?'

Logic in the face of Cristina's determination simply didn't equate. 'OK, so we check out the gown. On the condition we also look at something for *you*.'

Cristina offered a chuckle in amusement. 'Oh, no, you don't.'

'Hey. A deal's a deal.'

A waiter appeared, took their order, and Gianna sank back in her chair. It felt as if the last three years had disappeared like nothing as they resumed a friendship they'd previously shared whilst she had lived in Madrid.

'What's the situation between you and Raúl?'

This was Cristina, shooting straight from the hip, no preliminaries.

'I imagined business would keep him in Madrid.'

'While you're here in Mallorca? Are you mad?'

'You say this...*because*?

Christina viewed her carefully. 'You mean, you haven't figured it out yet?'

'I'm here because Teresa asked me to visit.'

'Tia Teresa's illness is very sad,' Christina agreed. 'It has touched us all.'

'*But?*'

'It is also opportune with time and distance to review the circumstances which prompted you to leave.'

There didn't seem any point in avoiding the issue. 'It won't change anything,' she stated, only to have Cristina's eyes sharpen.

'You do know Raúl filed stalking charges against Sierra?' One look seemed to convince her otherwise. 'No, I guess not.' She pursed her lips. 'He adores you. Always has.' She paused as she appeared to come to a decision. 'What the two of you share is special.'

Was, Gianna amended, only to have Cristina shake her head.

'Do yourself a favour and go seek the *real* truth.'

As if she could do that. The question was did she want to?

'OK, I'm done,' Cristina said smoothly. 'We have some serious shopping to do.' She offered a faintly wicked smile. 'Let's go flash some plastic.'

They did. The gown Cristina recommended was sheer perfection, in lilac chiffon, with tiny crystals beading a fitted bodice, thin spaghetti straps, and a softly flowing full-length skirt that showcased Gianna's slender form to attractive advantage. A matching wrap added a finishing touch.

'Now, was I right?' Cristina queried as they exited the boutique. 'Or was I *right*?'

Gianna laughed and lifted a hand to share a high-five gesture. 'I concede. Now it's *your* turn.'

Red—a powerful colour for a powerful young woman.

'Fantastic,' Gianna declared a short while later as Cristina checked her mirrored image. 'You *have* to have it.'

'You're *wicked*.'

Gianna merely smiled. 'If the glove fits...'

The *vendeuse* smiled at the thought of her commission on two expensive gowns, and carefully packaged each purchase in tissue before consigning them to a glossy signature carry-bag.

'Coffee—hot, sweet and strong,' Gianna directed as they emerged from the boutique. 'While *you* get to tell me about the Real Madrid soccer player.'

'Nothing to tell.'

'You don't see it going anywhere?'

'How can it? His face is constantly in the media. He doesn't make a move without some photographer trailing along in the hope of a photo opportunity.' Cristina gave a careless shrug. 'Who wants that?'

'You like him.' It was a statement, not a query.

'I'm merely one in a cast of thousands...millions,' she amended.

'You might see it that way,' Gianna offered sagely. 'The question is...does he?'

'Who would know?'

'Maybe he's tired of women playing the sycophant and he values your honesty.'

'And maybe the moon is just a round yellow cheese-ball.'

At that moment Gianna's cellphone beeped, and she took the message, keyed in an answer, then returned the phone to her bag.

'We have ten minutes before Miguel collects me.'

Except it was Raúl at the wheel when the large car slid to a halt outside the hotel entrance. Cristina declined his offer to drop her back to Aunt Rosita's apartment.

'Shopping,' she explained eloquently, then waved as Raúl eased the Mercedes into the flow of traffic.

'If Miguel was unavailable, I could easily have taken a taxi. There was no need for you to stop work.'

He cast her a brief musing glance. 'Perhaps I chose to take a break.'

'How kind.'

He bit down the desire to laugh. 'You managed to fit in some shopping?'

'Cristina can be very persuasive.'

'Girl-time?'

'Something a man will never understand.'

'Oh, I don't know. Men tend to bond with each other from time to time.'

'Business. The stock market. Shares. Property. Women talk clothes, shoes, bags, cosmetics, perfume.'

He negotiated an intersection, then drawled, 'You want to talk clothes?'

She turned and subjected him to an analytical appraisal. 'Love the shirt. That deep blue enhances the darkly brooding Mediterranean look.' She wasn't done. 'And the cologne…what is that? A special lux blend, or off the shelf?'

'Darkly *brooding*?'

'Oh, definitely. White also does it,' she offered sweetly. 'Perhaps you could try pale blue, or…' she paused fractionally '…pale pink? Just for a change, of course. Although I doubt your contemporaries would take you seriously in pink. Now, you can't beat a black tee to project masculinity. A thin cotton blend that hugs the shoulders, emphasises the biceps and hints at tight abs. Now, there's a *look*. Worn with black jeans, naturally.'

'Naturally.'

'Of course, if you want to go *all out*, you could let your

hair grow a little, just so the ends curl at your nape, but kept well groomed—although wild and unruly is also a captivating look. Women *love* to have something to grab on to in the throes of passion. I could consider a moustache, well trimmed, although I think kissing a man with one could be rather hard on the lips.'

'Anything else?'

'Don't wear a gold neck chain. They're so *yesterday*. A Rolex is a must. And I do like a ring that makes a statement. Platinum set with two rows of diamonds. Hand-crafted leather shoes. Preferably Italian.'

'What's wrong with Spanish?'

'Absolutely nothing. I'm merely offering my personal preferences here.'

'I would never have guessed.'

'You did suggest we talk *clothes*,' she reminded him with a sweet smile. 'I *could*, if asked nicely, assess your wardrobe.'

'There is nothing wrong with my wardrobe.'

'Of course not. If I recall correctly, everything is colour-coded—suits, shirts, ties, trousers, even shoes.'

'And that's a fashion crime?'

'Not at all. It merely accentuates your need for order. I, on the other hand, rather enjoy the seek and find method… I'm invariably surprised.' Not quite true, for she did keep everything together in neat groups. Besides, she could always put her hand on what she needed at any given time.

The Mercedes began to lose speed, and within seconds Raúl used a remote to open the gates to Teresa's villa.

'There, you see,' Gianna offered in a deceptively mild voice. 'We managed to survive the drive without once lapsing into an argument.'

His eyes gleamed with amusement. 'The day isn't over, minx.'

'If that's an endearment, it sucks.'

'What would you have me call you? *Querida? Amante?*'

'Please don't. They no longer apply.'

He drew the car to a halt beneath the *porte-cochère*, and she collected her package and slid from the passenger seat, supremely conscious of him as they passed through the massive double doors into the lobby.

'Thanks for the ride,' she said quickly as she made for the staircase.

'Think nothing of it.'

There were several hours until dinner, hours which she needed to fill productively, and somehow subsiding into a chair with a book held little appeal. The time difference meant it was too early to call Annaliese at Bellissima, and her brother, Ben, would be out taking his early-morning run.

She needed action of the physical kind—exercise that would use up her excess energy. A hard workout would do it, but she'd need to drive to the nearest gym...which was *where*?

Elena would know. She quickly changed into cotton trousers, pulled on a tee, then stowed shorts, a tank top, sneakers and her wallet into a backpack and made her way down to the kitchen.

'Of course, *señora*. I shall tell Miguel.'

Except instead of handing her a set of keys Miguel insisted on acting as chauffeur, in spite of her assurance all she needed were specific directions.

'The *señor* insists.'

'There was no need to disturb Raúl,' Gianna protested, only to incur a frown in dissent.

'I respectfully disagree. The *señor* insists you do not venture away from the villa alone.'

You have to be joking. Words she didn't express aloud. Instead, she merely inclined her head. 'Would you mind waiting? I need to discuss something with the *señor*.'

Did she ever!

The office door was closed, its heavy panelled door an imposing statement which failed to deter her from issuing one brief knock before entering.

Raúl glanced up from the computer screen, caught the determined look in those blue eyes, and settled back in his chair to view her with deceptive indolence.

On one level he was amused to discover she imagined she could do battle with him...and win. Yet her barely concealed anger was intriguing.

He was scheduled to participate in a conference call in five minutes, which didn't allow much time for the inevitable verbal tussle she intended to perform.

'Miguel has instructions to deliver and collect you from wherever you want to go.'

Her eyes flared. 'I don't *need* a bodyguard. And don't you dare refer to Miguel as anything else.'

He lifted both arms and crossed them behind his head as he regarded her thoughtfully. 'You'd prefer to drive to a destination you're unfamiliar with, perhaps even misinterpret directions and end up on a winding mountain road?'

He almost expected a verbally aggressive denial, and she didn't disappoint.

'I *lived* and drove a car in Madrid, remember?'

'Mallorca is not Madrid.'

'In which case I'll call for a taxi.'

'Doing so won't necessarily eliminate a possible confrontation involving media attention.'

He saw her eyes widen, then begin to narrow. 'What *precisely* are you saying?'

'Sierra is holidaying on the island.'

And hunting *him*.

Raúl shook his head. 'Think again.'

Her? Comprehension occurred swiftly as she envisaged a few scenarios Sierra was capable of manufacturing...none of which were pretty.

'And you were planning on telling me this...*when?*'

'After dinner, when Teresa retired for the evening.'

Gianna's gaze didn't waver. 'You believe Sierra will contrive a supposedly chance meeting...and you don't think I'm capable of handling her?'

'I'd prefer not to see you put in that position.'

She took a deep breath and expelled it slowly. 'Don't underestimate me,' she warned with silky intent. She longed to fling a verbal barb, only to restrain herself from doing so.

It irked that he knew, and her eyes flashed blue fire.

'My purpose is to prevent any mud-slinging Sierra may choose to create in order to gain the sort of attention Teresa would find distressing.' He paused imperceptibly. 'Not to mention *you.*'

'Oh, *please.*'

She was no longer the emotionally vulnerable young woman of three years ago. Yet his gut instinct warned he implement precautionary measures.

Sierra was unpredictable at best. A disturbed young woman who had played a deliberate game to which only legal action had brought surcease...by which time his marriage had been in tatters and Gianna had retreated to the other side of the world.

Sierra had been very clever, ensuring that while she skated to the edge of harassment she didn't cross it, choosing instead to use her family connections to gain invitations to social events he attended on the Velez-Saldaña conglomerate's behalf, thereby providing a visual taunt he was powerless to prevent while she abided by the terms of the restraining order. She didn't call, contact or approach him in any way.

She didn't need to, he reflected bitterly. The damage had already been done.

'Miguel or I will accompany you. Choose.'

Gianna didn't hesitate. 'Miguel,' she nominated sweetly, and glimpsed his faint smile as she turned to exit the office.

Working out helped ease some of the built-up tension, and when she was done, showered, changed and had alerted Miguel via cellphone that she was ready to return to the villa, she felt refreshed, alert and on top of her game… whatever her game happened to be.

Staying abreast of Raúl had to figure in there somewhere.

Let's not forget Sierra whose presence in Mallorca seemed to indicate she maintained a close eye and ear on every detail regarding Raúl.

Not exactly difficult to do, Gianna had to admit, when he regularly appeared in the news media, having successfully closed another deal, or attending a social event. Therefore it seemed feasible word had circulated that Gianna was also in residence at his mother's villa.

A young woman who had regained her emotional and mental strength…was *healed*, confident and strong.

So why did she feel emotionally connected to Raúl when she'd mentally confined him in a locked box and thrown away the key?

Sure she had. During the daylight hours.

It was the dark night hours when his image intruded into her dreams…taunting, haunting in a way that made for restlessness and little sleep.

It was almost frightening that she could still be attracted to him when he'd betrayed her with Sierra.

She had the proof…didn't she? Even though he'd denied the affair.

Except since spending time with him again in Mallorca a glimmer of doubt had intruded, causing her to re-examine for the umpteenth time the facts as she knew them.

Sierra visiting Argentina at the same time as Raúl had been in Rio on business. Coincidentally staying at the same hotel or so she'd said.

When Gianna had called him, it had been Sierra who had answered the phone in his suite.

But had Sierra arrived uninvited on some pretext or other as Raúl had assured her?

Had he, in fact, been taking a call on his cellphone, unaware Sierra had picked up the landline on the first ring?

Had Sierra dismissed the call as being in-house…as he had said?

Gianna had accepted the evidence as being conclusive proof…*sure* in her mind at the time that it was the truth. Except she'd been experiencing depression over the loss of their babe, vulnerable, sensitive and susceptible…and Sierra had been so convincing in her intention to wreak havoc.

Oh, God… What if she had been wrong? What if the entire debacle had been a deliberate attempt on Sierra's part to cause trouble?

Should she have believed Raúl's denial? Trusted in him? *Seen* the situation for what it was?

The thought she might have played into Sierra's hands sickened her now, as it had then. Dammit, she'd loved Raúl with every cell in her body, her heart, all that she was. Believed in him, *them*, the sanctity of their marriage.

Had he been faithful to her since they'd first met as he'd assured her?

Think, she cautioned. Only there was danger in too much thought.

She had a *life* in Australia, a home, business, friends… *plans*.

Yet the lingering doubt persisted, brought to the surface by Cristina's confidence, and no matter how hard she tried it wouldn't go away.

CHAPTER EIGHT

IT WAS during breakfast that Teresa mentioned a soirée to be held that evening in a friend's villa in the hills overlooking the Mediterranean Sea.

'It will be a pleasure to represent you,' Raúl assured her gently, in a bid to minimise Teresa's voiced regret at not being able to attend.

'Ana is incredibly generous in opening her home to host these occasions. My help is minimal in comparison.'

Yet Gianna recalled with ease the number of times Teresa had opened her Madrid home to host various fund-raising functions. The expense of doing so gifted without question.

Devising interesting functions in order to raise funds for deserving charities required experience, imagination, and above all, organisation. Committees were formed, women volunteered their time, expertise and even their homes in a bid to host a successful soirée to benefit a children's hospital wing with equipment, toys, digital televisions, DVDs. The list was endless, the functions many. Some were elaborate annual events; others by select invitation only.

Gianna had always respected the time and energy Teresa devoted to causes close to her heart, and knew the sadness

Teresa must experience now at being forced through illness to take a much less active role.

'Gianna, are you sure you don't mind partnering Raúl?'

Excuse me? Since when was it assumed she would partner Raúl? Surely there was someone else he could call on, even at such short notice?

Except how could she say she had other plans when *all* her plans centered around Teresa's welfare?

'Of course not,' she assured her with a smile.

'Thank you. I'm very grateful.'

And that was sufficient. After all, attending a function supporting a good cause was no big deal. It wasn't as if it was a new experience, given she'd attended similar functions in the past.

It was likely she'd be able to touch base with a few people she hadn't seen in a few years. Appearing at Raúl's side didn't make it a *date*. It just so happened she was visiting Teresa at the time.

Choosing what to wear posed no problem as she instinctively selected the lilac gown with its crystal beading.

The colour enhanced her blue eyes, added soft texture to her skin, and with the skilled appliance of make-up the overall result was pleasing.

The length of her hair was swept into a fashionable knot held in place with crystal pins. A light spritz of her favourite perfume, diamond ear-studs, a slim diamond tennis bracelet added a finishing touch, and she slid her feet into delicate silver strappy stilettos, collected an evening clutch purse, then she exited the room and made her way to the head of the staircase.

Raúl was in the process of descending, and he turned and waited for her to join him.

The breath caught in her throat—a habit which occurred far too often just lately for her peace of mind.

Resplendent in a black tailored evening suit, snow-white linen shirt with black silk tie, he was something else. Ruggedly attractive, with harshly chiselled features, well-defined bone structure, he emanated a formidable aura of power. For beneath his forceful image lay a blend of latent sensuality which drew women like bees to a honeypot.

Including *her*.

Even now, when she professed to dislike him for his purported transgressions.

'Beautiful,' he complimented quietly, and stilled the urge to place his lips against the sweet curve of her neck.

'Thank you.'

The faint pulse at the base of her throat had quickened its pace, and he took pleasure from the fact.

Miguel had the Mercedes parked adjacent the main entrance, and Raúl saw her seated before crossing round the vehicle to slip in behind the wheel.

'It would help if you'd fill me in about the purpose of this evening's function, the name of our host and hostess, and any applicable background information,' Gianna suggested as they left the villa.

'Ana and Franco own a spacious villa at Sóller, high on a hill overlooking the sea,' Raúl informed her. 'Ana is a tireless supporter of children's charities, especially those for children disadvantaged by life-threatening illness. Franco shared similar business interests with my late father, and both families are friends of long standing.'

'Tonight's function is specifically aimed at raising funds for which particular charity?'

'The building of an entertainment wing where terminally ill children can enjoy some of the luxuries most children take for granted. Electronic games that can be engaged in via remote control onto individual screens and played from their wheelchairs. Future donations will include a nurse-aide's salary. Laptop computers set up to access the Internet so that the children can e-mail family and friends. The aim is to stimulate the mind and keep it active, even if physical mobility is limited.'

Mallorca bore so much history, if one wanted to explore and research it, but it was the scenery that captured Gianna's interest. The tree-clad hills with villas peeping through the lush greenery. The many bays, beautiful beaches, the open sea. The horizon where the deep sapphire waters met with the azure sky, changing as the day progressed into night until the ocean and sky merged as one. The warm climate, the sun's heat that cooled as night darkened the sky. The sophistication provided by the wealthy, which vied with the tourists who visited to share in the idyllic lifestyle.

It held memories of happier times, when Teresa had based herself in Madrid and flown in to Mallorca for the occasional weekend. The few times she and Raúl had flown in for a relaxing few days.

'We're nearly there.'

She'd been lost in thought, and hadn't noticed the distance they'd covered, or Raúl's skilled handling as they ascended the winding road.

Minutes later he eased speed and paused at a set of closed ornate gates, where visual identification was established via his driver's licence and printed invitation.

It was a large property, spread out over several hectares, and already numerous cars lined the driveway.

Imposing and magnificent were only two superlatives Gianna accorded the large double-storeyed mansion. And that only related to the exterior.

Security guarded the entrance, where a further check

took place…and it was only afterwards Gianna fully understood why.

An auction of art and precious jewellery was the feature of the evening, and any amount bid over and above the conservative reserve would be donated to charity.

Items were on display in a separate room guarded by a security team. Items worth millions of euros, Gianna calculated at a guess as she browsed the locked glass display cases.

Each item bore the reserve price, and a catalogue tabling detailed description was handed to each guest.

'You are *kidding* me,' Gianna offered quietly, for the room resembled a very organised Aladdin's cave.

'Hence the written invitations delivered individually by hand.'

'Raúl, Gianna,' a gracious feminine voice greeted. 'How lovely of you to accept our invitation.'

'Ana, it's a pleasure.' Raúl brushed his cheek to each of hers, and Gianna found herself receiving a similar salutation from their hostess.

'Please adjourn to the lounge for drinks. There are plenty of refreshments, so please help yourselves. The auction will begin at ten.'

It was difficult to assess the number of invited guests… more than a hundred?

'Almost two hundred, I believe,' Raúl estimated, and smiled at her faint surprise, aware it irked her that he could read her so easily. 'Do you see anything you like?'

'There are so many exquisite items it would be impossible to choose any one.' Not to mention reserve prices *way* over the range of anything she could afford.

'What about you?'

'Yes.'

'That's it…just *yes*?'

He lifted a hand and trailed gentle fingers down her cheek. 'Why is it women are so curious, hmm?'

'It's our natural vocation.'

He uttered a husky laugh, and dropped his hand to rest at her waist. 'We'll go join the rest of the guests.'

It was easy to sip superb champagne, be tempted by a bountiful supply of finger food, and chat with guests she hadn't seen in three years. Not one of whom expressed surprise at seeing her coupled with Raúl.

Unlikely, she admitted, when he never left her side.

If there was masked speculation she didn't pick up on it, and for the first time she began to relax, to smile and let some of the tension ebb.

There was a sense of excitement when Ana and Franco announced the auction would begin, and a representative of the *policia* observed the proceedings while an accredited auctioneer took the podium. Security officers delivered each item, guarded it then removed it as successful bidders were noted by designated number and their bid recorded.

Although Gianna had attended similar events in the past, this one stood out as being spectacular. Every item received a successful bid, rising without exception to well above the reserve price.

Raúl obtained two items, each for a sum that made her swallow rather hastily. The first being a painting she'd briefly lingered to admire…an exquisite small portrait of a young girl from a previous century, lovingly entranced by the kitten she held in her arms. The second a beautiful sapphire surrounded by diamonds on a delicate gold chain, together with matching ear-studs.

Both Ana and Franco endorsed the auction's success, and announced a conservative figure of the funds raised for the nominated charity, whereupon they thanked their guests and invited them to enjoy themselves, while advising coffee would soon be served.

In hindsight, it might have been wise to leave at that point—although who could have predicted the last person on this earth Gianna wanted to see should put in an appearance?

Given Raúl's warning that Sierra was in Mallorca, it was only a matter of *when*, not if Sierra appeared on the scene, yet nevertheless it came as a shock to see her nemesis in the flesh, *here*.

With the security measures in place, where had she been during the auction—and, what was more…who was she with?

Did any of it *matter*?

Next question…had Raúl noticed her?

And if he had, what action would he take?

Worse, what were the legal implications if the restraining order he'd implemented was still effective?

Irrespective of which, Sierra possessed incredible nerve, risking much to appear here tonight in what had to be a calculated move to confront.

Who was the target? Raúl or her? *Both?*

Who knew?

It was difficult to appear dispassionate as she met Sierra's deliberate gaze. The young woman looked exquisitely groomed in a designer gown that hugged every curve. Dark blond hair had undergone a change and was now much lighter with subtle streaks, in a style that framed her features to perfection.

Fascinated, Gianna couldn't help wondering if Sierra deliberately practised numerous poses in front of a mirror in order to gain maximum effect. The smile, the eyes… *blue*, when she could have sworn she remembered them as being hazel…contacts, perhaps?…the flutter of her hand, the light tinkling laughter.

The woman was a work of art…artifice, that was.

Most red-blooded men would be drawn to her, curious perhaps to discover if she delivered the sensual promise evident in the packaging.

Gianna had to give it to her…Sierra played her hand well. She was accompanied, she saw now, by a partner who resembled a male model for *GQ* magazine. Someone Sierra had hired as her date for the night? Without question someone who had scored an invitation.

Hush your mouth, Gianna silently chastised herself… Let's not digress into pettiness. The woman could have changed.

Sure, and little pink piglets might fly!

It was interesting to view Sierra with a fresh perspective, noting the acquisitive behaviour, the determination… not love, but the desire to *possess*. At any cost? Uncaring if her actions, her words, might destroy a relationship, a marriage?

Had that been Sierra's original goal? Perhaps even veering towards the psychotic: *If I can't have him, no other woman will*.

Gianna met Raúl's direct gaze, and offered a wry smile.

'Impossible you haven't noticed Sierra has crawled out of the woodwork. One assumes there is a purpose to her presence here tonight?'

'Without question.'

'You must be flattered.'

'No.'

She arched an eyebrow. 'Really? A beautiful woman prepared to do *anything*…' she trailed deliberately.

'No,' he reiterated quietly.

'Why not?'

He threaded his fingers through her own and lifted them to his lips. 'She isn't you.'

For a moment she just looked at him, unsure whether he was playing for real…or just *playing a part*.

Flippancy was the only way to go. 'Is this where I look at you with adoration?'

'It wouldn't hurt.'

'I'm sadly out of practice.'

'I can help with that.'

He lowered his head and brushed his mouth to her temple, lingered there, then placed an arm along the back of her waist and drew her in to his side.

'You're verging on overkill,' she warned sweetly, and saw the edge of his mouth curve a little.

'You think this is a game?'

'It isn't?'

His eyes darkened, and his features lost any pretence at humour. 'No.'

Raúl caught the momentary confusion evident before she successfully tamped it down, and he silently cursed, aware how carefully he needed to tread if he was to achieve a successful resolution.

In business he called the shots, issued ruthless terms and was prepared to walk away if those terms were not met.

But this was personal. Very personal.

'Sierra seems to be heading this way.' And was doing so gracefully, pausing here and there to speak with an acquaintance. In order to detract from her true purpose? Gianna pondered, only to reluctantly admire the young woman's perspicacity…for when it came to dedicated purpose, Sierra won hands down.

Battle, undoubtedly, was about to commence.

'Raúl. *Querido.*'

Wow, how did she manage to inject so much seductive innuendo into so few words? *Practice*, Gianna deduced. Whatever, it was incredibly effective, and she unconsciously held her breath for his response.

There was none.

Oh, my. In seeming slow motion she caught the dangerous glitter in Sierra's eyes, then it was gone, and the perfectly painted mouth widened a little, then formed a moue.

'Not even *hola*, Raúl?'

Gianna spared him a surreptitious glance, then wished she hadn't as a shiver slid icily down her spine at the hardness evident in his dark gaze.

Total cut-off, no communication whatsoever…and none intended.

Not once had she ever witnessed such pitiless disregard. Not even at the height of their verbal controversy over Sierra's assertions in the final days before she'd left him.

No way in the world would *she* want to be subject to such chilling resolve from *anyone*. Should she ever incur such a look from Raúl, she'd simply curl up and die.

Not, however, Sierra, who shifted her attention briefly to Gianna.

'So…what prompted you to return? His billions? Or his ability to make you feel like the kind of woman no other man can?'

Oh, boy. She held Sierra's vindictive gaze, and evinced quietly, 'I'm in Mallorca at Raúl's request.'

If looks could kill, she'd be dead.

'Has he offered you an obscene amount of money to try again for a Velez-Saldaña heir?' She conducted a deliberate examination from head to toe and back again. 'Raúl should move on to a woman who is fertile.'

The words stung, as they were intended to.

'Another word,' Raúl issued in silky warning, 'and I'll ask Security to remove you.'

'You can't do that, *amante*. I'm here with a partner who has a genuine invitation.' With a cruel smile, she returned to Gianna. 'I wouldn't have failed to give him a child…as you did.'

Hurtful parting words, which speared Gianna's heart as Sierra intended. She was barely conscious of the soothing slide of Raúl's hand as it moved from her waist to rest at her nape.

'We'll leave.'

She turned, her eyes large in the paleness of her face. Except he glimpsed innate strength there, the faint smile that surely cost her.

'And give Sierra the satisfaction of knowing a deliberate barb found its mark? I don't think so.'

'Then let's move out onto the terrace.'

Gianna didn't resist as he indicated one of several French doors, and she crossed to the ornate balustrade to admire the nightscape. They were high in the hills, with a panoramic view towards Palma with its sprinkling of lights, and beyond the black mass of the ocean.

There were stars, and a light breeze wafting in from the sea.

Relaxing, and infinitely serene, she acknowledged as she breathed in the fresh air and felt the tension Sierra had generated began to ease.

Raúl stood at her side, and she didn't protest as he drew her close. There was comfort in his touch, a warm strength that made her want to bury her cheek against his chest.

Almost as if he knew, he curved a hand over her nape and pulled her in, then rested his cheek against her own in an intimate gesture that reminded her so much of what they'd used to share.

·

It felt good…so good she didn't want to move, and she gave a faint sigh in protest as he caught hold of her chin, lifting it so she had no recourse but to look at him.

There was a wealth of emotion evident in the depth of his eyes, and she swallowed the slight lump in her throat as he lowered his head and brushed his lips to her forehead, trailed to her cheek, then sought her mouth in a gentle kiss that subtly changed as she became powerless not to respond.

It was like coming home…to a place she instinctively knew she belonged.

For endless minutes she gave in to the pleasure, the hard feel of his arousal a potent force as he shaped her body, drawing her in until she became lost, wanting so much more and she barely disguised her groan as Raúl began to ease back.

'We have company,' he said quietly, close to her ear, as she lowered her arms from around his neck and turned slightly to see their hostess regarding them both with amused benevolence.

'I hope this is what I think it might be?' Ana queried with a smile.

Gianna uttered a whispered, *'No…'* Only to have Raúl bestow a light kiss, then stifle any further protest by pressing a finger to her mouth.

'Querida, how long did you imagine we could keep it quiet?'

Was he *insane*?

'You have decided to reconcile?' Ana posed with delight. 'Teresa will be so very happy with the news. Let me be the first to offer congratulations to you both.'

'Gracias.'

What was he doing? A kiss…that was all. Sure, a tiny

voice taunted. *You were close to* devouring *each other. And enjoying it.*

Ohmigod. This wasn't happening. She was lost in a dream from which she'd soon awake.

Except the scene was startlingly real, and she blinked rapidly as if to clear her mind.

'We must all share a celebratory drink,' their hostess bade cheerfully as she indicated the French doors.

Gianna's denial rose and died in her throat as she gave Raúl a beseeching look that had no effect whatsoever.

You can't do this.

Did she speak the words aloud?

Apparently not. And seconds later she stood in the doorway, anchored close to Raúl's side, with their hostess calling for everyone's attention.

Say something. Anything. Just stop this farce before it begins.

Except the words wouldn't form…and then it was too late.

'I have a special announcement to make. It is my great pleasure to inform you that my dear friends Raúl and Gianna Velez-Saldaña have decided to reconcile. Let us all wish them well, and drink a toast to their future.'

Champagne appeared, and staff quickly assembled flutes and distributed them among the guests.

Somehow Gianna managed to smile as guests she knew and some she didn't came by to express their good wishes… Even Sierra leaned in close and voiced in a hideous whisper, *'Watch your back. It doesn't pay to be too clever.'*

Gianna barely refrained from a pithy rejoinder, aware silence was the better option.

Raúl was a constant presence, playing the part a little too well. A vivid reminder of how it had used to be between them. The musing smile that promised much once they were alone. A light touch of his hand at her waist the trail of his fingers down the length of her spine to rest low and brush back and forth in a gentle movement guaranteed to stir her senses.

Revenge, when the opportunity presented itself, was sweet, and she uttered a few words so quietly he angled his head down to catch them.

It would have appeared to any onlooker as an endearing moment…except the light brush of her mouth hid the deliberate nip of sharp white teeth to his earlobe.

Only *she* caught the faint hiss of his expelled breath, and glimpsed the sudden dark gleam in his eyes promising retribution.

Eventually the evening drew to a close, and Gianna waited until the car cleared the gates before turning towards him.

'Explain, *please*,' she demanded with barely controlled anger, 'why you didn't correct Ana's assumption?'

The mountain road was narrow by any standard, winding, and required concentration.

'I was more concerned in protecting you.'

His slightly amused drawl merely ratcheted up her anger another notch.

'Don't toy with me. I'm a hair's breadth away from *hitting* you.'

'At least wait until we're off this road before you try.'

She bit her lip to restrain the words she longed to hurl at him. Words which flowed the instant Raúl reached the main route leading to Teresa's villa.

'What in *hell* were you thinking back there?'

'In reference to…?'

She shot him a venomous look which would have felled a lesser man. 'We are *not* reconciling.'

'Then perhaps *you* can explain why you were totally *with* me in every sense of the word.'

The thing was *she had been*…so totally lost she'd had no awareness of anything except *him*.

Be honest. She'd wanted to tear his clothes off and eat him alive.

'So, you kiss very well.' It was a totally inadequate protestation, and she heard a husky sound emerge from his throat that sounded suspiciously like subdued laughter.

'You choose to imagine that's all it was? Sensual expertise?'

No, she admitted wretchedly. It was so much more than that, and the knowledge blew her mind.

'Yes.'

The car slowed and he used a remote to open the gates, then again to open the garage. As he cut the headlights, the garage lights sprang on and the exterior door folded down.

In one smooth movement he released his seat belt and turned towards her.

'Liar,' Raúl accused quietly as he cradled her face and covered her mouth with his own.

Her initial protest died as he coaxed her lips apart and began exploring the soft tissues with gentle expertise.

Warmth invaded her veins, firing her nerve-ends until she felt every cell bloom sensually alive, and with a faint sigh she simply gave herself up to the magic only he could create.

The kiss deepened, becoming more urgent, and she was barely aware of his hand caressing her thigh while the other shaped her breast.

She was unaware of her hands reaching for him, sliding the buttons free from his shirt as she sought warm skin and taut musculature.

'Let's get out of here.' Deep husky words filled with passionate intent as he slid free from the car, then crossed to the passenger side and drew her unresisting to her feet.

A faint gasp left her throat as he slid an arm beneath her knees and swung her into his arms.

'Put me down,' she protested weakly as he entered the foyer and carried her upstairs to her suite, then closed the door behind them.

Heat pulsed through her veins, setting her body on fire… for him, only him. The sane, *sensible* part of her issued a silent warning her emotional heart chose to ignore. She *needed* this, *him*, with every breath she took, and she defied rational thought as her hands sought to remove his jacket, loosen his tie, then tear hurriedly at the buttons on his shirt…aware he was equally bent on dispensing with her clothes.

Skin, just skin…warm, fluid muscle and sinew. She revelled in the feel of him, the clean male musky scent mingling with the exclusive tones of his cologne.

His hand trailed low over her stomach and sought her moist heat, the acutely sensitive clitoris…he sensed her intake of breath as he skilfully brought her to orgasm.

Eroticism at its pinnacle…shameless and wildly primitive…and at that moment she couldn't *see*, only *feel*, with the desperate need for fulfilment.

More. She wanted so much more. *Now*. It had to be now, or she'd die.

She linked her hands at his nape and in one agile movement straddled his hips, instinctively arching in against his arousal as he cupped her bottom to hold her there.

His mouth sought hers as he invaded the inner depths, searching delicate tissues, savouring the taste and feel of her…teasing the highly sensitised heat as he moved her against the length of his arousal…until she closed the edge of her teeth over his tongue in silent urgency for his possession.

Which he gave, positioning her as he slid in carefully, stilled, then thrust in deep…absorbing her cry as he held her there, aware her heartbeat thudded in unison with his own.

It wasn't enough… He wanted her in bed, under him, at his mercy as he drove her wild.

A few steps was all it took, and he disengaged, tore back the bedcovers in one easy movement, then tumbled them both down onto the sheeted mattress.

His mouth sought the sensitive curve at the edge of her neck, then traced a path to her breast, moistened the tender peak and drew it into his mouth. He heard the breath hitch in her throat as he tugged hard, and he softened his touch as her nails pressed into his biceps.

Not content, he trailed light kisses to her waist, lingered at her navel, then with lazy appreciation moved slowly down to settle at the apex of her thighs.

Her body quivered as he blew gently against the sensitive flesh, then sought the honeyed cleft, traced it with the tip of his tongue, bestowed an open-mouthed kiss… Then he sought the satiny entrance and delved deep, only to retreat and graze the clitoris until she shattered beneath his touch.

With one easy movement, he shifted and began trailing soft kisses down one inner thigh to her knee and back again, before inching slowly to her breast.

Her hands, which had been digging into the mattress, moved to clasp his hips…and it was *he* who felt the breath hitch in his throat as she enclosed his arousal, stroked him, then eased to cup him.

'Careful, *querida*,' he warned her gently as he nipped the swollen peak with the edge of his teeth…only to chuckle quietly as she grasped his head and dragged his mouth to her own in a kiss that took passion to new heights.

It was then he entered her in a slow, deep slide that drew a soft moan from her throat as her muscles tightened, gripping him as she urged him to quicken the pace, demanding as he lost himself in deep, powerful thrusts that rocked them both as they soared high…so high. She simply held on as he took her to the edge, suspended her there, then tipped her over in a glorious free-fall that left them both dragging breath into their lungs.

Sated, and deliciously replete, she held him close, murmuring indistinctly as she rested in his embrace.

His, indisputably *his*.

As he was *hers*…had been from the first moment he had laid eyes on her. She'd intrigued him…he who'd become jaded with the women of his acquaintance. Mostly sycophants who imagined being attractive arm candy and receptive in bed would gain them entry into his world…for a time.

Gianna had been different. *Alive, sparkling*…unutterably sweet, and honest, with a dry wit he'd found remarkably refreshing. No hidden agenda, and equally at ease with his high-powered lifestyle. She'd taught him to lighten up, to laugh a little…and to love with his heart, his soul.

He'd proposed, gifted her his ring, for marriage had been a given…just a matter of organising a day, a time.

Her accidental pregnancy had delighted him, precipitating the wedding. But the unforeseen miscarriage had been followed soon after by Sierra's damnably false innuendos… and Gianna had slipped to a place where he'd been unable to reach her.

'Sleep,' he bade her gently, and he watched her lashes drift down.

'You should leave.'

He pressed a light kiss to her temple and nestled her close in against him. 'Later.'

Except it was she who stirred in the early pre-dawn hours to the light trail of his mouth as he nuzzled the hollow at the base of her throat. She who uttered little protest as he made love to her again…a slow, gentle loving that was all *her* pleasure, after which he scooped her into his arms and carried her into the *en suite* bathroom, where he shared her shower, teasing her with the soap before gifting it to her to return the favour.

Which she did, so caught up in the thrall of him and what they'd shared that she refused to *think*.

This…*this* was heaven. The beautiful aftermath of good sex. *Very* good sex. *Intimacy* at its most rapturous, when the heart was gloriously alive…and free from intrusive thought.

If only it could remain like this, Gianna pondered a trifle wistfully. To be able to go back to the place before it all went wrong…to view it from a different mind-set and avoid the pain and bitterness.

A hollow laugh rose and died in her throat.

So much for not thinking.

'*Don't,*' Raúl chided gently.

She didn't pretend to misunderstand. 'It's impossible not to.'

He caught hold of her chin and tilted it so she had no recourse but to meet the darkness in his eyes. 'There has never been anyone since you. No one.'

No one? Not even…

Dared she believe him…*trust him*? At the time of their marriage she would have given an unequivocal yes.

Now, even discounting Sierra's damning words to the contrary, it seemed almost impossible to comprehend a man with Raúl's sexual energy could remain celibate for such a long period of time.

There were so many layers to remove to reach the kernel of truth, she perceived.

Sex…even very good sex…did little more than temporarily paper over the cracks.

Which brought forth the question…*had* she been wrong three years ago? So distressed and emotionally traumatised that she'd chosen to believe Sierra's accounting instead of trusting Raúl?

It was something she'd agonised over countless times, only to reach the same conclusion…logic in favour of an unlikely truth.

Did she possess the *nous*, the courage, to confront Sierra and shoot down each and every purported fact…and verify it as fallacy?

She had the rest of her life in front of her…a successful business, a pleasant apartment, a good lifestyle.

All of which she'd trade in a heartbeat…

Oh, God.

She closed her eyes, counted to ten, then slowly opened them again.

Don't let intimacy cloud an important issue, she cautioned herself silently as Raúl released her and closed the water dial.

With ease he caught up a towel and hitched it at his waist, then he filched another and gently blotted the moisture from her body.

Towelled dry, he drew her into the bedroom, straightened the covers, then slid beneath them and gathered her in.

The remembered closeness of being held like this…the soft drift of his fingers as they trailed her spine…the way one hand cupped her head and the slide of his lips to her forehead…it was like coming home to a place where her body instinctively knew it belonged.

CHAPTER NINE

GIANNA drifted awake, reluctant to leave what she perceived to be an exquisite dream, only to fail as she became slowly aware of her sprawled position in the bed when she usually woke curled on her side.

She yawned, stretched a little…and felt the sexual pull deep within. For a brief moment she stilled, then groaned.

Raúl.

Ohmigod, they hadn't…

She lifted her head and saw the empty space he'd occupied, became aware the scent of his cologne still lingered and weathered the memory, *in detail*, of what had transpired through the night.

Hell.

The time? She picked up her watch and did a double-take to see it was almost nine.

She never slept in—well, let's qualify that. She hadn't had *reason* to sleep late for a long while.

Time to rise and shine, shower, dress and greet whatever the day might hold, she decided as she gathered up fresh clothes and headed for the *en suite* bathroom.

Twenty minutes later she entered the dining room to find Raúl and Teresa enjoying breakfast.

'Good morning.'

Gianna met Teresa's warm smile with one of her own, and returned the greeting while studiously avoiding Raúl's thoughtful gaze.

'Do help yourself and join us.'

The *chiffonier* held juice, cereal, yoghurt, fresh fruit, coffee, and she made her selection, then crossed to take a seat at the table.

It was impossible not to be supremely conscious of Raúl's close proximity. Nor to dismiss the vivid memory of his recent possession. After a long absence from sexual activity she could still *feel* his imprint deep within…a constant vivid reminder in her mind.

Could anyone *tell*?

Hell, she hoped not—especially Teresa, who would undoubtedly read more into it than Gianna was prepared to admit, even to herself.

And *Raúl?* Was it her imagination, or did she glimpse an indolent gleam in his dark gaze as he focused it on her for a few overlong seconds before returning his attention to the food on his plate?

'I feel quite well this morning,' Teresa announced with a pleased smile. 'Sufficiently so to accept a dear friend's invitation to lunch. Miguel will drive me.' She turned towards Gianna. 'It would be lovely to have you join me.'

Her response was immediate. 'It'll be a pleasure.'

'Adriana is delightful,' Teresa continued. 'A true friend of long standing. You have met her, of course.'

So she had, at various fundraising functions in Madrid before and after her marriage to Raúl. An exotic beauty, who had chosen to age gracefully, and whose generosity to select charities was legend. Disadvantaged and terminally ill children won Adriana's unstinting time and support, Gianna recalled.

Raúl finished the last of his coffee, placed the cup onto its saucer before leaning back in his chair and engaging Teresa's attention.

'There is something you should hear before it becomes public knowledge,' he began quietly, and Gianna's eyes widened in consternation.

He wasn't…*surely*? Yet on some level she realised Teresa would learn the news soon enough, and better for it to come from Raúl than for his mother to hear it secondhand.

'Last night, it was assumed our attendance together indicated a reconciliation, and an announcement was made to that effect.'

Teresa's eyes, which had initially brightened, assumed a thoughtful expression. 'Which is not true?'

Raúl took hold of Gianna's hand and threaded his fingers through her own, felt their slight pull, and tightened his grip a little. 'It's what I hoped we could work towards, given sufficient time.'

Teresa turned towards Gianna. 'How do you feel about this?'

Oh, my. Blatant honesty wasn't an option. Consequently she aimed for ambiguity. 'There are some unresolved issues.'

'I love you both dearly,' Teresa offered with genuine affection. 'Nothing would please me more than to see you reunited.'

'*Gracias*, Madre. If you'll excuse me?' Raúl rose to his feet and brushed his lips to Teresa's temple. 'I'll be in the office.'

Gianna offered a slight smile, only to have her eyes widen as he crossed to her side and rested his hand briefly on her shoulder. 'Enjoy your lunch.'

It was such a light gesture, and one that could be interpreted merely as a kind courtesy. So why did it feel as if pink coloured her cheeks in damnably sensitive reaction?

'Thank you,' she managed with ease, and wondered if she was the only one to glimpse the momentary amusement apparent in his dark eyes before he turned and walked from the room.

'There are a few items of jewellery I very much want you to have,' Teresa began gently. 'They were to be bequeathed to you in my will, but now that you are here I can gift them to you personally.'

Distress clouded Gianna's eyes, and she placed a hand on Teresa's arm. 'Please,' she protested, 'I can't accept anything.'

'Nonsense. It would mean so much to me, knowing you have them.' She withdrew a slim jeweller's case and set it on the table. 'Open it, my dear.'

'Teresa…'

'They're yours,' she said simply. 'Allow me the pleasure of gifting them to you.'

Gianna's fingers trembled a little as she released the clasp, and her eyes widened at the sight of a beautiful diamond bracelet in an antique setting.

'The bracelet was handed to my mother by her mother, and my great-grandmother before her. A gift, I believe, to her by a member of the Spanish aristocracy.'

'I can't possibly…'

'Yes, you can. There are matching ear-studs, and a dress ring.'

Collectively, they had to be worth a small fortune, and Gianna's features creased with concern.

'You have Cristina…'

'Cristina will receive her share. But these,' she declared as she retrieved the bracelet, 'are special, and they are for you.'

'Raúl…'

'The gift has his approval.'

There was little she could say except, 'Thank you. I shall treasure them.'

'I know. The very reason I chose them to gift to you.'

Gianna rose to her feet and bestowed a gentle kiss to Teresa's cheek, then enfolded her in a careful hug. 'Thank you.' Any minute soon she'd lapse into tears.

Perhaps Teresa sensed emotions so close to the surface, for she smiled and stood to her feet.

'Let's take a walk through the grounds. It's a lovely day, and the gardens are so pretty at this time of year.'

True, Gianna acknowledged as they took the lift down to ground level and stepped out into the sunshine.

Beautifully groomed lawns, a paved walkway, attractive stone fountains, and carefully tended garden borders featuring carnations, chrysanthemums, gerbera daisies, lilies and lovely asters.

It was pleasantly warm, the skies a clear blue, and there was a relaxing timeliness in listening to Teresa explain the history of the island.

'I adore being here. It's so peaceful away from the tourist area. A fresh breeze drifts in from the ocean, and there are luxury amenities to be had within easy distance. I have a few friends here, and the pace of life is less frenetic than in Madrid.' She cast Gianna a smile. 'There was a time when I enjoyed a busy social existence. The parties, the theatre, various charities to whom the Velez-Saldaña conglomerate chooses to lend its support. The luncheons, dinners the fundraising committees.' She paused to point out a fabulous display of roses. 'Beautiful, aren't they?'

Indeed they were…deep reds, brilliant yellows and luscious pinks.

'Now I prefer a quiet life, sharing as much time as

possible with my son, a few special friends…' Teresa paused and offered a genuine smile. 'And you,' she added gently.

Gianna found it impossible to still the sudden lump that rose in her throat.

A short time, Raúl had imparted. *A few months, at most.*

The medics had to be wrong. To believe this wonderful gracious lady's diminishing health would take her from this earth before her rightful time seemed a tragedy.

'I admire you,' Gianna opined gently.

Teresa didn't pretend to misunderstand. 'Someone said it before me…*first you cry.* My dear, I did that in the beginning.' Her dark eyes sparkled with humour. 'It served no purpose. Instead I chose to make each day count.' A light laugh escaped her lips. 'And I do, believe me.'

Gianna paused and gave Teresa an impulsive hug, then stood at arm's length. 'I want you to know how much I care for you.' She blinked against the threat of tears…and won. 'You've always been there for me. Even in the not-so-good times. Thank you,' she said simply.

Teresa was silent for several long seconds. 'You are as much my daughter as if you were born to me,' she declared gently.

Oh, dear heaven… Unshed tears shimmered in her eyes, and this time she lost as they welled and spilled over to run in slow rivulets down each cheek.

Emotional overload.

A night with Raúl in her bed, very little sleep, her mind and heart in a state of turmoil, together with Teresa's avowal of affection it was almost too much.

'Am I to assume the reconciliation announcement was pre-empted by circumstance?' Teresa posed quietly.

There was no question in evading the truth. 'Sierra was a guest last night.'

'Ah.' Teresa expelled a breath and linked Gianna's arm through her own. 'Sierra is a dangerous young woman.'

'There was an…incident,' Gianna revealed, reluctant to relay the hateful words Sierra had uttered.

'Raúl chose to defend you?'

You could say that. 'Yes.' The terrace came vividly to mind—how it had felt to be drawn into his arms…the kiss…dear heaven, *magic*. As if the past three years no longer existed. For at that moment the slate had been wiped clean. There was only passion…and the need to fulfil it.

Did Teresa guess there had been an aftermath?

How could she not?

'Your happiness must be paramount,' Teresa said gently. 'There are occasions in one's life when love is tested. Believe me when I say I will support whatever decision you choose to make.'

'Thank you.' Any minute soon she'd resort to tears again, and that would never do.

Almost as if Teresa sensed her emotional turmoil, she impulsively caught hold of her hand. 'Come, we will examine Miguel's garden. He is so proud that everything is organic.' She gave a light laugh. 'Elena is only allowed to pick the vegetables and salad greens he permits, and then it must be beneath his eagle eye.'

They were so caught up in the moment they were unaware that Raúl had risen from behind the desk and was unobtrusively observing the scene from the office window.

Two women, a generation apart.

His mother, of average height and slim, her shoulders held straight, the wig she wore so much like her own hair there was no detectable difference.

Gianna, his wife, in direct contrast, with her petite stature, slender curves and blond hair.

Together they shared a common unbreakable bond. Linked irrespective of their connection to him.

Soon…far too soon…he would lose one of them. As heartbreaking as that would be, he had no intention of allowing Gianna to slip through his fingers.

Last night…even the thought of what they'd shared through the dark hours was enough to incite arousal. *Need*, he accorded wryly. Rampant primitive passion for one woman…the *only* woman with whom he connected on every level. Mind, body, spirit. An essential part of him. As much as the air he breathed…his life force.

Did Teresa know?

How could she not? For it was she, more than anyone else, who had witnessed his drive to expand the power he wielded in the global market during the past few years. And he'd succeeded, even surpassing his own unrealistic goals as he'd poured all his energies into winning huge contracts, exacting takeovers, restructuring in a way that had trebled the Velez-Saldaña holdings.

Yet in a way his hands were tied…loosely, he conceded. In the business arena he could afford to be ruthless…put an unnegotiable deal on the table and walk away if it wasn't accepted.

A wry smile curved his lips. *This…Gianna…*was personal, requiring a vastly different strategy. One he couldn't afford to misdirect if he wanted her to share the rest of his life.

He watched as the two women linked arms and continued along the path. He paused contemplatively until they moved out of sight, then resumed his position behind the desk, pulled up data on screen and resumed essential work.

* * *

Choosing what to wear to lunch required thoughtful consideration, Gianna posed as she checked the selection of clothes she'd brought with her.

Teresa possessed impeccable taste in everything, and her wardrobe consisted of exquisite wear designed for every possible occasion.

Dress-up time, Gianna decided as she donned a beautifully tailored dress in deep aqua, added matching stilettos, then tended to her make-up, fixed her hair in a smooth twist and attached a slender gold chain and gold studs to each ear. A spritz of her favourite perfume, and she was good to go.

Miguel delivered them to a beautiful mansion in Portals Vells, set in landscaped gardens with spectacular views of the sea.

Adriana Ramirez de Arroyo greeted Teresa with fond affection and turned towards Gianna.

'My dear, how lovely to see you. Do come and join the other guests in the *sala*.'

The room encompassed nine guests…women whose wealth and social status rivalled that of their hostess. Three of them Gianna recalled having met at one charity function or another in Madrid.

Introductions completed, Gianna accepted a light orange fruit spritzer in an exquisite crystal goblet, took a sip, and found it to be delicious.

Genuine friends, mostly similar in age, with a long history together, Gianna realised as they chatted and laughed prior to moving into a beautiful formal dining room and being seated for lunch. Pleasant, charming women, content in their own skin, with no apparent need for pretence of any kind.

No fewer than five courses were served by staff, each dish a visual and epicurean feast. Light instrumental music provided an unobtrusive accompaniment, and it proved delightful to witness Teresa's pleasure.

'Teresa adores you,' Adriana imparted gently as they lingered over coffee. 'It is good you are here to spend time with her.'

'She's a very special lady.' The words came straight from Gianna's heart.

'We've known each other for many years,' Adriana relayed. 'Shared time together, watched our respective children grow, succeed and marry.' A soft smile curved her lips. 'Teresa will be overjoyed with news of your reconciliation with Raúl. She loves you.'

What else could she say except, 'Thank you…'

'It has been Teresa who has accompanied Raúl to various functions in your absence.'

Gianna hid her surprise quite well…or so she thought.

'My dear, you were unaware of this?' Adriana paused a little. 'Then possibly you do not know Raúl has chosen to represent Velez-Saldaña alone on the occasions when Teresa's failing health has prevented her attendance.'

Teresa hadn't mentioned it in any of her letters. But then Raúl's mother possessed sufficient wisdom to accept her son was eminently capable of managing his personal life.

Did time heal? Was it possible to find a resolution?

Perhaps…

Oh, for heaven's sake…what was she thinking?

She'd moved on. Made a new life for herself. *Dammit*, she enjoyed what she'd achieved. What was more, she hadn't touched a *cent* of the money Raúl authorised each month into her bank account. Hadn't she notified him via his bank to cease payment? Not that he'd taken any notice.

Yet…last night…

Don't go there. It was just *sex*…albeit very good sex.

That it had reawakened her emotions and attacked the very core of her soul was immaterial, for it didn't change his infidelity.

Except for the tiny core of doubt seeding in her mind.

'Shall we adjourn to the *sala*?'

A concerned glance was all it took to discern Teresa was beginning to tire. Gianna discreetly checked her watch. It was three-forty-five, and Miguel had instructions to collect them at four-thirty.

The car arrived promptly, and hugs were exchanged as Adriana accompanied them to the *porte-cochère*, where Miguel ensured Teresa became comfortably seated while Gianna crossed to the other side and slid into the adjoining seat.

It had been a pleasant afternoon, and Gianna said as much as the car traversed the driveway.

Teresa reached out and took Gianna's hand in hers. 'Lovely,' she agreed. 'Thank you for accompanying me.'

'The pleasure was all mine,' she responded quietly.

They shared a comfortable silence during the drive to Teresa's villa, and once indoors Teresa acknowledged her nurse and the need to rest.

Gianna gave her an impulsive hug, then watched as Teresa ascended the stairs to the gallery and moved towards her own suite of rooms in the west wing.

The hours stretched ahead…hours in which she could access e-mails, check the online data Annaliese would have posted. Reading presented another option, but she felt a need to expend some restless energy, and the thought of stroking lengths in the pool held definite appeal.

It didn't take long to change, don a bikini, collect a towel and make her way to the smoke-tinted glass-roofed pool.

Grateful for the solitude, she dived into the cool water and struck out, frequently changing style as she powered length after length before switching to a more leisurely pace.

'Are you done?'

Gianna stilled at the sound of that familiar drawl, and turned to see Raúl standing with relaxed ease on the wide expanse of marble tiles surrounding the pool.

How long had he been there? She hadn't heard a sound, nor had she noticed his presence.

'What if I say no?'

'I'll take that as an invitation to join you.'

She cast his tall frame attired in black trousers and white shirt a sweeping glance. 'You're not suitably dressed.' *Undressed*, she added silently, and glimpsed his faint smile.

'I don't recall it being a problem in the past.'

No, it hadn't been. 'This is Teresa's home,' she managed with a degree of reproval, and felt her eyes widen as he unbuttoned his shirt, discarded it, then he released the zip fastening on his trousers, slipped off his shoes, socks, and disposed of all three.

Black silk briefs separated him from total nudity, although the effect of his barely covered frame caused her pulse-rate to quicken to an alarming beat as he surfaced in the pool mere inches from where she trod water.

Dark and dangerous, was her initial reaction, and her lips involuntarily parted as he cupped her face and smoothed a thumb over one cheek.

'How was lunch?'

'Fine.'

One eyebrow lifted in silent query, and she held his gaze with equanimity.

'Adriana is a wonderful hostess,' she relayed with deliberate patience. 'The guests proved to be delightful company. Superb food.'

'Teresa?'

She sobered a little. 'Teresa appeared to enjoy herself immensely,' she opined quietly. 'Although she tired as the afternoon progressed.'

'Hence her decision to have a light meal on a tray in her suite.'

'You think the afternoon may have been too much for her?'

He didn't respond immediately. 'I think she deserves to choose how and with whom she spends what time she has left.'

'I'm so sorry.' Such simple words, meant to convey so much, and his eyes darkened as a slight shiver shook her slender frame.

'Cold?'

It was more than that. A chill she couldn't explain. For it was enmeshed in a host of emotions she felt unable to voice. Paramount was the need to seek solitude…for to remain here, *close* to him, was more than she could bear.

'I need to go change,' she managed lightly, grateful when he released her, and she swam to the side of the pool where she lifted herself in one easy movement onto the marble tiles.

It took bare minutes to towel the moisture from her body and fix the towel sarong-style round her slender form, then she picked up a second towel and wound it turban-fashion over her hair.

Without a backward glance she entered the adjacent cabana and made her way through to the guest wing and her suite, where she showered, washed her hair, then donned comfortable jeans, a knit top, and opened her laptop.

If she'd had a choice she'd have opted to follow Teresa's lead and eat a light meal here, instead of joining Raúl in the dining room. Dinner *à deux* didn't exactly appeal for a number of reasons…too many to settle for any *one*.

Consequently she changed into black silky evening trousers, added a black lacy top, fixed her hair, applied light blusher and lipgloss, and slid her feet into black stilettos.

Informal, almost casual, but with a degree of style, she accorded, and made her way downstairs.

'Señor Raúl will join you soon,' Elena imparted as Gianna entered the dining room.

So much for hoping to dine alone. Which, given the intimacy they'd shared, seemed little less than *ridiculous*.

So suck it up and *pretend*.

Sure, and she could *do* that?

Try, a silent voice prompted.

And she did…she really did.

Except Raúl was *there*, a disturbing, disruptive presence who stirred her emotions to fever-pitch. Even to observe his hands as he ate proved a vivid reminder of just what havoc those hands could cause to her equilibrium…

As to his mouth…she didn't dare go there.

'I may be needed in Madrid tomorrow.' He forked the last morsel of food and pushed his plate to one side. 'A conference call in this instance isn't achieving a satisfactory result.'

Gianna set her plate aside, half the contents untouched… attempting to do the food justice was out of the question.

'In that case you should give whatever it is your personal attention.'

He leaned back in his chair and regarded her thoughtfully. 'You've been like a kitten on hot bricks and eaten little. Care to offer a reason?'

OK, he'd asked. *Tell him.* 'Last night was a mistake.'

'I disagree.'

He knew—of course he knew what bothered her. How

could he not, when he had always been able to read her like an open book?

'I don't *do* casual sex.'

'There was nothing casual about it.'

Why had she started this? It was *insane* to think she could best him in any way.

'It's not going to happen again,' she vowed firmly.

'It's a woman's prerogative to decline.'

And she hadn't done that, had she? Instead she'd invited him in, urged him on...with each successive occasion.

Why? Stupid question. She knew precisely what had motivated her...need, electrifying passion, and a compelling urgency to experience sexual chemistry at its zenith. With him...only *him*.

Gianna stood to her feet. 'If you'll excuse me?'

He made no attempt to stop her, other than to offer quietly, 'Avoiding the issue won't make it go away.'

Perhaps not, but she didn't have to stay and cross verbal swords with him.

Not the most successful evening, she accorded as she entered the beautifully tiled foyer and headed for the staircase.

If only she could turn the clock back twenty-four hours... except that wasn't possible.

So get over it, she chided herself as she entered her suite and discarded her clothes for cotton sleep trousers and a sleep tank before moving into the adjoining *en suite* bathroom.

Minutes later she emerged and crossed to the bed, slid beneath the covers and reached for a book.

She managed to read two pages without absorbing so much as a word, and she was about to return it to the nightstand when the bedroom door opened and Raúl entered the room.

Gianna's eyes widened with disbelief. 'What are you doing?' Words momentarily failed her. 'I'm not having sex with you.'

'Your call,' he drawled with indolent ease, and began unbuttoning his shirt. 'Sleeping is fine.'

CHAPTER TEN

'IF YOU think you're sharing my bed...' She trailed off as her anger began to heat as he discarded his shirt, then freed the zip fastening on his trousers. 'It's not going to happen.'

She escaped the bed as he slid into it, and without thought snatched up a pillow and threw it at him.

He caught it easily, and she gritted her teeth as he returned it to its original position.

'You want to play?'

'*No.*'

'Then, unless you intend standing there indefinitely, I suggest you get into bed.' For a long moment he regarded her in silence. '*Sleep* is the operative word.' He waited a beat. 'Together.'

Gianna wanted to stamp her foot like a recalcitrant child, and hated that he knew it. 'You're an arrogant *fiend.*' She could think of worse words to hurl at him, and almost did.

'Careful, *mi mujer,*' Raúl warned her softly, and glimpsed the sudden gleam of anger in those deep blue eyes a second before she snatched up the pillow and *thumped* him with it.

Her forward momentum worked against her, and the next instant she lay sprawled on top of him. His hold was loose, although the expression evident in those dark eyes mere inches beneath her own was sufficient to send warning bells clamouring through her body.

One false move would be all it would take, and while anger urged her to struggle against him the sane, rational part of her dictated commonsense.

'Let me go.'

He didn't move or attempt to release her, and she wavered on the brink, momentarily uncertain...of him, herself and how the situation would evolve.

'Please.'

For a moment she was unsure whether he'd comply, and she gasped as he cradled her head and brought her mouth down to his in a possession that rocked her very being.

Passion, in all its many facets...pulsing, mesmeric, intensely primitive. It took hold of her emotions and swept her to a place where there was no coherent thought...only the man, his touch and its cataclysmic effect.

She was dying here...a wild and wanton supplicant prepared to *beg*.

'Please.'

It was all he needed. Restrictive nightwear became discarded as he positioned her to accept him, and she held on as he took her for the ride of her life...and *his*...as rapture sent them spiralling high to reach that exquisite magical place in perfect accord.

It was almost more than she could bear, and she rested against him, too enervated to move as erotic sensation began to subside.

She was conscious of the light trail of his fingers along the edge of her spine, soothing gently as he murmured softly in his native Spanish... A few words registered on some remote level, and his lips caressed her temple, then rested against her cheek.

'Sleep, *querida*,' Raúl directed huskily.

His voice was the last thing she recalled, and when she woke in the morning his side of the bed was empty. She reached out a hand and found the sheets cool to her touch.

There was no sound of the shower running in the *en suite* bathroom, and it was then she remembered he had business to deal with in Madrid. A quick check of the time revealed it was after eight, which meant he was probably at the airport, if not already in the city.

The day loomed ahead—one which she intended to devote entirely to Teresa who, if she felt sufficiently well enough, might appreciate a drive…perhaps even a pause for some light refreshment.

With that thought in mind, Gianna slid from the bed, indulged in a leisurely shower, then dressed in casual white cotton trousers, added a colourful knit top, and ran lightly downstairs.

'My dear, let's venture out a little this morning,' Teresa suggested as they lingered over coffee. 'I rested well yesterday and enjoyed a good night's sleep.'

'I'm in,' Gianna assured her with a warm smile. 'Where would you like to go?'

'Jardines de Alfàbia,' Teresa enthused. 'I'm particularly fond of the Moorish gardens surrounding the old manor house. The house itself is set amid lemon groves, and there are splendid beds of roses. A garden lover's idea of heaven.'

Miguel drove them north of Palma, less than twenty kilometres distant, and Gianna experienced a sense of awe as she wandered the footpaths shaded by pergolas, with streams and a number of softly murmuring fountains. A stately avenue of plane trees led to the house—formerly a residence of the Mallorcan kings, Teresa informed her, according to history.

However, it was the gardens themselves, the many beds of beautiful roses, which caused the breath to catch in her throat.

'Splendid, are they not?'

Perfect blooms, emerging buds, provided a riot of colour.

'It's so peaceful here,' Gianna offered. 'Serene. An idyllic place for writers, poets, painters to meditate and create.'

'Not during the tourist season,' Teresa began with a faint smile. 'But for now, at this time of day, it is lovely. I like to come here to be inspired, and to be reminded life continues and evolves.' She spared Gianna a look that held mild humour. 'Occasionally I ask Miguel to walk with me and we discuss...' She shook her head. 'No, we *argue*, politely of course, about what we shall introduce with the new planting. It occasionally becomes a lively debate.'

'Which you invariably win,' Gianna teased, and Teresa laughed.

'Not always. But then, life would be very dull without a certain conflict of interest, don't you think?'

'I can't imagine anyone wanting to argue with you.'

'Raúl chooses to call it a reminder of wisdom whenever we clash, which is rare. He is very patient with me.'

They wandered for a while, pausing here and there to admire one of the many fountains, an ivy-clad wall, a large plane tree which offered shade.

There was time to pause for light refreshments before returning to where Miguel waited with the car. It had been a pleasant sojourn, one which had obviously delighted Teresa.

Following lunch, Gianna retreated to her suite, while

Teresa rested, and checked her laptop, read the latest update Annaliese had sent via e-mail and switched her mindset to business. Sales were steady, and most of the ordered stock had arrived on time, with the exception of a few items held up by Customs. Gianna frowned, then keyed in a response with who to call. The delay was irregular. So, too, was the request by the clerk for Gianna to deal with it personally. For some reason it appeared items addressed to Bellissima were being withheld from clearance.

Very frustrating, given the client was anxiously waiting for the package. Annaliese's polite insistence that *she* was relieving manageress during the owner's absence didn't appear to carry much weight.

Which meant Gianna would need reference numbers, dates, in order to make a personal call. With the time difference, there was no chance Annaliese could access the information needed until she reached the boutique several hours from now.

It was perhaps as well it was only a matter of days before she'd be back on the Gold Coast and available to keep a vigilant eye on business.

Apropos of which, she should consider shopping for a few gifts to take back for Ben, Eloise and the children. Not forgetting Annaliese, who was doing a sterling job with Bellissima in her absence.

While most of the boutiques would be closed, the large department stores in Palma remained open. A few hours was all she'd require, and she went downstairs in search of Elena, who in turn contacted Miguel's cellphone, and arrangements were made to leave within half an hour.

A change of clothes, her hair pulled back in a small ponytail, a scarf, sunglasses, carry-bag, wallet and cellphone and she was good to go.

'I'll be fine,' Gianna assured Miguel as he pulled in to a parking bay. 'I'll call you in about two hours, OK?'

'Not OK. I will accompany you. Señor Raúl's instructions.'

She looked at him carefully. 'Do you *really* want to traipse around a department store?'

'It is my job.'

To argue seemed pointless, and she waited while he secured permanent parking, then, with Miguel at her side, she searched for appropriate gifts. A much-favoured perfume for Eloise, a pictorial book on Inca history for Ben. The children scored tees and books, while it took a little longer to find something for Annaliese. Bracelets, thin, several of them in multi-colours...perfect.

An hour and a half later Gianna declared she was done... only to pause at a display counter with crystal, jade and rose quartz ornaments. Delicate, exquisitely carved miniatures. But it was the crystal rose which drew her attention. It shot prisms of light as it moved on an individual turntable, and she didn't hesitate.

It was the perfect gift for Teresa, and she listened to the salesperson's patter about the quality and workmanship, even down to the pearl of dew on one of the leaves.

Satisfied, she accompanied Miguel to the car, and when they reached the villa she thanked him before running lightly upstairs to her suite, where she changed into a bikini, filched a towel, then sought the pool.

A light breeze teased the air as the sun sat high in a cloudless sky, revealing the panoramic vista beyond, with colourful stucco villas bearing multi-coloured terracotta roof tiles, and exotic flora and fauna down to the distant cerulean blue ocean.

With care she dived into the sparkling water and stroked several laps, before resting her arms against the pool's tiled lip as she took time to appreciate the peaceful serenity apparent, the relaxed atmosphere.

So why did the thought of leaving cause a pang of… *what?* Surely not *regret?*

She couldn't *want* to stay. It wasn't only not possible… it held disastrous consequences to her emotional heart.

Because nothing from the past had been resolved…not at the time, nor could it be now.

Why not? a rational inner voice queried.

She'd taken on board the words of a vindictive ex-lover prepared to use any means to reach an ultimate goal. *Listened* to Sierra, and discounted Raúl's explanation because the incident had occurred at a time when she was an emotional mess, and Sierra's version had appeared more *plausible?*

But…*what if Raúl's explanation had been the right one?*

Why hadn't she stayed to check it out for herself instead of escaping to the other side of the world and the only familiar sanctuary she'd imagined she had?

The benefit of hindsight could be a mixed blessing, she perceived ruefully, for it forced her to choose between accepting the *status quo*…or beginning a search for the irrefutable truth.

With Raúl in Madrid on business, and Teresa resting, it was an ideal opportunity to make some investigative enquiries as to what had *really* happened almost three years ago.

She could, she ruminated, leave it be.

But, *dammit*, she'd reached a point where she *needed* whatever proof she could unearth in order to resolve the incident conclusively…irrespective of the result.

Gianna had no problem recalling the name of the hotel where Raúl had stayed in Rio, for it had been indelibly imprinted in her mind from the onset together with the dates.

Who could forget the momentous event of a husband's infidelity? The date, time and place where it took place?

Purportedly, she allowed, surprised she could even consider the distinction.

As a precaution she used her cellphone instead of the villa's landline, and with a list of written questions she made the first call.

By day's end she'd made several connections, researched media archives online…and accumulated sufficient information to reach some interesting…make that *intriguing* conclusions.

Enough, she determined, to confront Sierra.

It was just a matter of where and when…preferably in private.

Almost as if fate played a helpful hand, there was a phone call from Teresa's friend, Adriana, reminding Teresa of an invitation to a fashion showing the following afternoon in order to raise funds for terminally ill children. The event would begin with lunch.

Teresa seemed pale when she joined Gianna for dinner, and ate little. And although she dismissed feeling unwell she nevertheless begged tiredness soon after dinner, and at the nurse's bidding excused herself and retired for the evening.

Gianna opted to view a movie on DVD, and when the credits had rolled she accessed her laptop, caught up on a few e-mails, checked the data Annaliese had sent through, then made ready for bed.

She told herself she enjoyed the solitude and knew she lied. For all it had taken was a few nights of Raúl sharing her bed for her to miss his presence.

Admit it…she enjoyed having his hands on her body,

his mouth taking erotic liberties that made her forget everything except *him* and what he could make her feel.

What a conundrum…to want, but not accept she wanted or needed him. Except it was a truth she had to face—especially *now*, when she'd uncovered proof of Sierra's lies.

The question of what she was going to do with that proof, and how she intended to resolve the situation, conjured up various scenarios which played in her mind until sleep tipped her into a dream-like state, where the past merged with the present, providing stumbling blocks she fought hard to circumvent.

It was late when Raúl entered the villa after a tense day of negotiations, ending with his ultimatum that could swing the deal for or against the Velez-Saldaña conglomerate. It was a deal he wanted but on his terms.

He could have stayed in Madrid overnight. Common sense had dictated it to be a sensible option. Except he'd called his pilot and directed him to file a flight plan to Mallorca.

The reason was the sleeping form of his wife, curled beneath the bedcovers, blissfully unaware of his presence.

He shed his clothes, took a leisurely shower, then, towelled dry, he crossed to the bed and carefully slid in beside her.

She didn't stir as he gently gathered her close, and he pressed his lips to the sweet curve of her neck, then closed his eyes and attempted to sleep.

Gianna woke next morning as Raúl was in the process of fastening buttons on his business shirt.

His eyes gleamed with a degree of humour as he met her slightly bemused look. 'You slept like an angel.'

'Must have,' she acknowledged as she reached for her robe. 'I didn't even know you were here.'

'Is that a complaint because I didn't wake you?'

Her response was swift...too swift. 'No, of course not.'

A husky laugh escaped his throat as he crossed to her side and closed his mouth over her own. When he lifted his head she caught the wicked gleam in his eyes.

'Tonight, *mi mujer.*'

'You're returning to Madrid today?'

'*Sí.*'

She opened her mouth to ask why he hadn't stayed in his apartment, only to close it again as he touched a light finger to her lips.

'A lonely bed, *querida*, when I can be here with you through the night?'

Oh, my. A painful ache settled in the region of her heart. In a few more days her two-week sojourn here would conclude, and she'd board a flight out of Madrid for home.

Except the lines had become blurred, and she was no longer sure where *home* existed.

A week ago, it had unquestionably been Australia.

Now... Well, now it would be a wrench to leave Mallorca, Spain, and everything they meant to her. And Raúl... Dear God. *Leaving him would be the hardest thing she'd ever do.*

She became conscious of his studied gaze, and she curved her lips to form a winsome smile. 'Should I be flattered?'

He made an indistinguishable sound in his throat and reached for her, his mouth a seductive force as he took her own in a kiss that captured her soul and branded it his own.

Earth-shattering, primitive and totally shameless.

Her entire body seemed to coalesce as she gave herself up to him, for everything faded and became meaningless. There was only him, and electrifying passion.

She was barely conscious of him dispensing with her sleep tank until he shaped her breast and sought the tender peak with skilled fingers.

Sensation arrowed through her body, and a silent groan caught in her throat as he lifted her high and replaced his fingers with his mouth.

More, she needed *more*, and she gave an audible moan of distress as he gentled his touch, then relinquished it as he lowered her to her feet.

For a moment she was incapable of speech, and her eyes widened measurably as he cradled her face.

'Tonight, *querida*.'

She watched in mesmerised silence as he released her before tending to the buttons on his shirt, then he fixed his tie and shrugged into his suit jacket.

Gianna found her voice as he turned towards the door.

'Travel carefully.'

Raúl cast her a dark musing look over his shoulder. 'Always.'

Then he was gone, and she stood transfixed for several long seconds, still lost in an emotional vortex, until common sense exerted itself.

She needed to shower, dress, join Teresa for a leisurely breakfast, and then spend time with her.

Not long after that it would be time to get ready to attend the charity fashion show in Teresa's stead.

Gianna chose a chic fitted black lace dress with three-quarter sleeves and a scalloped hemline that reached just below her knees. The neckline showed just the right amount of cleavage.

Black stilettos, a minimum of jewellery, and understated make-up with emphasis on her eyes completed the look, and she caught up a small red clutch, checked the contents, then made her way downstairs to the foyer, where Miguel waited to drive her to the venue in Camp de Mar, near the picturesque port of Andratx.

The mansion was large, luxurious, and a testament to the host's extreme wealth. No expense had been spared with the floral decorations—exotic displays which had to have cost a fortune.

Adriana came forward with a genuine smile as Gianna entered the foyer.

'My dear, so good of you to come. I am sorry to hear Teresa is not having the best day. Let's go into the lounge and I'll introduce you to the guests.'

Superb champagne was offered as they mingled together, and while there were some men present, the majority of attendees were women...each of whom was exquisitely attired, perfectly coiffed and cosmetically beautiful.

A surreptitious glance was all it took to determine Sierra was not among them.

There were a few guests she'd met before, some of whom had been present at Adriana's home.

A certain competitiveness existed among the social elite...the fashionistas who flew to Paris and Milan each season to buy their clothing and shoes from top designer houses, flashing black Amex cards gifted by their wealthy husbands and lovers.

Except when it came to supporting worthy charitable causes they did so with unstinting generosity.

It was late afternoon when their hostess requested the guests' presence in the adjoining ballroom, set up with a professional runway and numerous tables precisely placed, with chairs sheathed in white linen caught at the back with an elaborate bow.

Gianna was pleased to discover she was sharing a table with Adriana, together with a pleasant woman whose name temporarily escaped her.

'Luisa,' was offered with a mischievous smile. 'We have met before, in Madrid, at a function you attended with your husband.'

'Of course.'

An impish gleam lightened her eyes. 'I've had a little work done, changed my hair colour, and now wear contacts.'

Gianna couldn't help but return the smile. 'You'd never know.'

'New husband, new image.'

Waitstaff began serving wine, together with platters holding a sumptuous selection of finger food designed to tempt the most discerning palate.

The hostess presented a short speech lauding the charity and informing them what funds were needed to add a wing to an existing facility.

Teresa had gifted a certified cheque as a donation, which Gianna had handed the hostess on arrival, and now she focused her attention on the runway as a DJ began spinning discs.

The first selection featured resort wear, and five models paraded the runway with practised flair.

It was during the second selection that she felt a light touch to her arm, and she turned slightly as Adriana warned quietly, 'Sierra has chosen to make her entrance.'

Flamboyant in red stiletto heels, flashing jewellery, and appearing cosmetically perfect, Sierra fluttered a hand in general greeting and made her way to the one remaining vacant seat at an adjoining table.

Gianna felt her stomach clench a little, and dismissed it as nervous tension. She'd coveted the opportunity for a confrontation, and now all she had to do was initiate it.

Verbal swords...*when*? After coffee, perhaps?

The confrontation occurred when Gianna elected to use one of the guest powder rooms to freshen up. She was in the midst of applying lipstick when the door opened and Sierra sauntered across the room to pause at her side.

'There's no place for you here.'

Gianna deliberately applied a final sweep of gloss to her lips, then she turned towards her nemesis. 'You have sole use of a designated guest powder room?'

'You want me to spell it out for you?'

'Not particularly.'

'Go back to where you came from,' Sierra directed with vengeful intent.

Calm... She could do cool and calm. 'If I choose not to heed your advice, what will your *modus operandi* be this time?' Her eyes hardened. 'Another *surprise* such as you planned in Rio?'

'I don't know what you're talking about.'

'Then I shall tell you.' Gianna lifted a hand and began by ticking off on her fingers. 'You were registered as a guest in the hotel hosting a high-profile fashion show *three blocks* from Raúl's hotel. The booking was made by you personally, paid for via your credit card, together with other relevant charges which included breakfast for *one* both mornings during your stay, as well as mini-bar and telephone charges.' She didn't give Sierra the chance to deny it, as she continued to count off each verified item. 'Media coverage tabled an intense round of meetings, together with photographic evidence of Raúl closing a multi-billion deal on behalf of the Velez-Saldaña conglomerate. While *his* hotel bill also showed room service charges for *one*.' She was on a roll. 'What's more, he checked out a day earlier than scheduled.'

Sierra's eyes glittered with malevolence. 'So how do you explain my presence in his suite?' she posed sweetly. 'If you recall, I answered his phone.'

'Coincidentally logged at the same time Room Service delivered Raúl's meal,' Gianna enlightened. 'A little too convenient, don't you think?'

'What a vivid imagination you have.'

'His cellphone statement logged a call made at the same time you picked up on a logged call from me to his suite's phone line.' She paused momentarily and her eyes darkened. 'Raúl threw you out, but the damage was already done.'

Sierra's features assumed an unattractive bitterness. 'My goodness, you *have* been busy.'

'Facts I should have checked three years ago.'

'Except you didn't, did you?'

'No,' she admitted evenly. A fact which had worked to Sierra's advantage. 'Much to my regret.'

'Raúl is *mine*.'

A vicious, almost obsessive statement, which raised faint warning bells to Gianna to pull back. 'You were his lover for a few brief months,' Gianna conceded, and saw the fashionista's eyes flash with fury.

'It should have ended in marriage.'

'Except he didn't propose,' Gianna reminded. 'And when he broke off the relationship you refused to accept it was over.' She drew in a deep breath and injected her voice with deliberate intent. 'Go focus your attention on someone other than my husband, and cease making a fool of yourself.'

They weren't just *words*. She meant every one of them.

Emotionally, passionately… *Trust, love,* in all its facets. The forever kind.

Dear heaven, had she ever stopped loving him?

Perhaps, for a while. When hurt, anger and disillusion had won out. Caused, she admitted, by Sierra.

For a moment irrational fear overtook her at the thought of losing him again, and resolve gave credence to determination. *Nothing…no one…*would come between them again. She'd make sure of it.

'Or?' Sierra demanded.

'I'll go public with the information I have.'

Sierra's eyes gleamed with malevolence. 'You wouldn't dare.'

'An interview with one of Spain's leading magazines,' Gianna informed her. 'Raúl is a prominent figure. I'm sure a journalist would delight in getting an inside story on our reconciliation. What caused the marriage to break down.' Her eyes hardened. '*Believe* I would confide all.'

'I'd sue.'

'Any lawyer worth his reputation would advise against it, given the proof I can supply.'

'If you mention my name…'

She aimed her final dart. 'I won't need to.'

A statement which drew uncontrollable rage from Sierra, and a hefty push which sent Gianna crashing against the marble vanity, immediately followed by a punch to her solar plexus.

'*Bitch.*' The word was accompanied by a few other choice expletives designed to blister the ears. 'I hope you rot in hell.' With that Sierra whirled and exited the powder room, leaving Gianna bent over in pain and gasping for air.

Not nice. In fact, she could add a few choice words of her own…when she got her breath back. Which at the moment seemed unlikely anytime soon.

It took a while to regain her composure before she returned to the ballroom and the table she occupied.

'My dear,' Adriana offered with concern, 'you're quite pale. Are you feeling unwell?'

Just a little physical and verbal altercation. 'I'm fine.' *Sure you are.* Coffee…hot, sweet and strong. Then she'd alert Miguel she was ready to leave.

The fashion show was winding down, with the final segment already being paraded down the runway. Glamorous evening gowns in soft floating chiffon…floral, block colours, stark black. Each a masterpiece in creation.

It was early evening when Gianna slid into the rear passenger seat with Miguel at the wheel. There was a sense of relief…even satisfaction…at how the afternoon had panned out.

Well, she could have done without Sierra's *physical* reaction, but at least she'd won the verbal battle. It made the painful bruising almost worthwhile.

Teresa seemed brighter after a restful day, and Gianna changed into comfortable clothes, then joined Teresa for a light meal, together with an account of the afternoon, the fashions, the guests, the total funds raised.

'I'm delighted the afternoon was such a success.'

'Adriana asked me to convey her best wishes.'

A warm smile curved Teresa's mouth. 'Adriana is a very kind friend.' She glanced up as the nurse entered the room. 'Ah, here is my fierce angel to ensure I take my medication on time.'

'*Fierce* and *angel* don't really equate.'

Teresa stood to her feet in one easy movement. 'Believe me, she is both.' There was fondness apparent that belied the words as she bade Gianna goodnight.

It wasn't late, and Gianna felt too restless to sleep. She checked e-mails, picked up a novel only to discard it.

A leisurely shower appealed, and she took her time, then, towelled dry, slid into bed and closed the light.

The afternoon played over in her mind as she recalled every word both she and Sierra had uttered.

Could she have handled it differently? Been more assertive? Perhaps. Yet she'd reiterated all the facts in sequence facts she'd elicited directly from the source, leaving Sierra no room to manoeuvre.

CHAPTER ELEVEN

GIANNA must have fallen asleep, for the next thing she remembered was being drawn into a deliciously evocative dream where her skin burgeoned into exquisite life with the erotic drift of a mouth bent on seduction.

A soft, throaty purr escaped her throat, and she instinctively arched her body in languorous acceptance, like a moth to flame, exulting as tantalising lips sought sensitive hollows and caressed vulnerable curves.

If this is a dream, please don't let me wake up just yet.

Except a small shaft of pain penetrated her subconscious, removing the veil of sleep and bringing with it an awareness of the dimly lit bedroom, the large bed…and the man sharing it with her.

'Raúl.' His name emerged from her lips as a soft sigh.

'Tired, *amante*?' His mouth shaped her own in a persuasive prelude as he sought the sweet moist cavern and began teasing her response. 'I can…'

'If you think I'm going to lie here…' she trailed off huskily, angling her mouth so it took possession of his own with wicked sorcery. 'Besides,' she managed when she broke contact to look deep into dark eyes heavy with sensual intent, 'you've already done most of the prep work…'

Her mouth curved into a seductive smile. 'Unless I was lost in a beautiful erotic dream?'

He shifted her to sit astride him, then cradled her head and brought it down to his own. 'What do you think?'

Real, very real, Gianna acknowledged as he reclaimed her mouth. And she used her body to tantalise his arousal… until he groaned, positioned her to accept him, then took her. Primitive, momentous…exhilarating. And so much more as he held her gaze with smouldering intensity. Sensation spiralled high, and he caught the moment she reached the peak…held her there as he joined her, tumbling them over the brink in a glorious sensual free-fall.

For what seemed an age she just drank him in, loving the feel of him deep inside her…the hard, fast beat of his heart against her hand, and knew it matched her own.

'Beautiful,' Raúl said gently as he drew her down to rest against him, and she felt the light drift of his fingers as they traced her spine.

It was this post-coital aftermath that caused every bone in her body to melt…a special time where the true meaning of intimacy held them bound together in sensual thrall, too enervated to move, yet so in tune with each other they were *one*…mind, body, and soul.

With care, he framed her face and took her mouth in a lingering kiss, then he nestled her head beneath his chin. 'Sleep, *querida*.'

Gianna murmured something indistinct as she closed a hand over his shoulder and slid into blissful oblivion.

The early-morning sun edged towards the horizon, turning the night's darkness to a shade of grey where shadows loomed and there was little definition in the landscape.

Gianna stirred, contemplated going back to sleep, only to discard the notion as she slid naked from the bed and crossed to the *en suite* bathroom, where she activated the shower and stood beneath the hot pulsing water.

Delicate rose-scented soap filled the air as she distributed it over her skin, and she winced a little as she encountered the swelling at the rear of her pelvis where Sierra had slammed her against the marble vanity.

Any day soon she'd be sporting a sizable bruise there.

Not to mention the midriff area, where she'd taken a killer punch from the vicious out-of-control woman.

Would Sierra retreat now, or would she scheme to instigate another ploy? *Who could know?*

Gianna was about to rinse off when the glass door slid open and Raúl stepped in. It was easy to smile, for she adored his early-morning look of rumpled hair, unshaven and dangerous.

Unclothed, he was something else. Broad shoulders, honed musculature chiselled to perfection. It was his arresting facial features, the wide-set dark eyes, wide cheekbones, and the faint grooves slashing each cheek that deepened when he smiled, laughed.

Tight butt, she added…and met the amused gleam in his slumbrous eyes.

'Are you done?'

Looking at him? She wanted to laugh, go to him and wind her arms up around his neck, then tease… *Just admiring the merchandise.* And invite his kiss, as she had many times.

Except this was *now*…not *then*, and she felt a degree of reservation, which was crazy given the intimacy they'd recently shared.

'I'll leave you to it.' Calm words that belied the way her insides began to curl at the lazy appreciation evident in his gaze.

'Stay.' He scooped up the soap and began smoothing

it over her shoulders with gentle strokes, despite her faint protest. 'You'd deny me this?'

No. It felt so good, so incredibly intimate, she almost closed her eyes as her body swayed slightly beneath his touch.

He cupped her breast, shaped it, then skimmed his knuckles over the tender peak…and felt the faint tremor skim her body.

He moved to her midriff, saw her flinch, and his hand stilled. 'You're hurt?' When she didn't answer, he caught hold of her chin between thumb and forefinger and tilted it so she had to look at him. 'Tell me.'

'I bumped into something. It's nothing.'

His eyes narrowed slightly and became dark. '*Who*, Gianna?' When she didn't answer, his voice assumed a silky drawl. 'Or shall I make a calculated guess?'

'Sierra was among the guests at the fashion show for charity I attended on Teresa's behalf yesterday afternoon,' she admitted, and glimpsed a muscle clench at the edge of his jaw.

'And?'

'We had a verbal altercation.'

She became conscious of the steady water flow as it beat down on their bodies. The delicate rose scent…

'Sierra *hit* you?'

Punched me, actually. 'Sort of.'

'What else?' Raúl dispensed with the soap and ran his hands over her ribs, stomach then he moved to her back, caught her indrawn breath as he touched her hip and uttered a vicious oath as he examined the slightly swollen area beginning to show the first tinges of a nasty bruise. 'Gianna?'

'I came into contact with a vanity unit in the powder room.'

His eyes hardened.

'She didn't like what I had to say.'

'And that was?'

Gianna gave him a condensed version, watching as his expression assumed pitiless disregard for the woman who'd sought to destroy his marriage.

'You would have carried through with your threat?'

Her eyes never wavered from his own. 'Not without informing you of my intention. But, *yes*,' she indicated firmly. 'Sierra's lies and manipulative behaviour have caused enough damage.'

So they had. Damage he'd attempted to repair, with little success.

To believe Gianna had sought to discover the truth for herself and confronted Sierra with a litany of fact almost undid him.

To have gone to such lengths meant she *cared*, and with *care* there was the hope he'd regain her trust.

Relief lightened his heart as he closed the water dial, picked up a towel and dried the moisture from her body before tending to his own.

He removed two towelling robes, helped her into one before selecting another for himself.

With considerable care he took hold of her hand and lifted it to his lips, his eyes dark and unfathomable. 'You should never have allowed yourself to be alone with her.'

'Sierra is an adult, not a child who throws a tantrum because she can't have what she wants. What were her parents thinking, indulging her by allowing such behaviour?'

'I imagine she fooled them as successfully as she managed to fool me.'

A hard act to maintain for three months, Gianna admitted, only to reveal her true nature when the idealistic

bubble burst. She could imagine how it had gone down…
the tears, the pleading, the machinations.

There was never going to be a better time to reach
him.

'I owe you an apology.'

His eyes sharpened and became incredibly dark.
'For?'

'Not believing in you,' she said simply.

For a long moment he simply looked at her, seeing the
shadows, the ethereal quality she strove to hide beneath
the surface…and his heart twisted a little at the pain she'd
suffered as a result of one woman's vindictive psychosis.

Without a word he swept an arm beneath her knees and
carried her into the bedroom, where he sank down into a
comfortable chair and settled her on his lap.

'Sierra played her cards a little too well by initiating
a game she could never win. At least not with me.' He
captured her face and his eyes seared her own. 'I failed to
see through the façade she presented until she mentioned
she should move in with me. It didn't go down well when
I chose to end the relationship. Polite refusals to take her
calls resulted in a false claim of pregnancy which I personally ensured was negative by insisting on independent
testing. When I threatened legal action, she promised she'd
never contact me again.'

Facts Gianna hadn't known. But then why should she
have? It had happened before she'd met Raúl, and formed
part of his past.

'Except Sierra turned up at the same events,' Gianna said
quietly, and felt his hand smooth gently over her head.

'Yes. It was awkward in that her father is a colleague
and mixes in the same social circles.'

How could she forget the number of times Sierra had accompanied her widowed father, always perfectly groomed,

a new designer gown shaping her slender curves, showcasing her generous cleavage? *There*, a visible personage designed to silently taunt the one man she coveted…a man who had, in her eyes, wilfully discarded her.

'Sierra saw a chink in your armour when you miscarried, and she sought to drive a wedge between us in the only way she knew how…by contriving a situation that would attack you at your most vulnerable.'

And she'd succeeded.

'You think it didn't hurt me to lie next to you each night and know you wept silent tears and couldn't sleep?'

Pain was evident, and regret. 'It killed me,' he revealed quietly, 'to witness your miscarriage. To know there was nothing I could do to help other than be there. And after you left, nothing I could say would ease the hurt Sierra had inflicted. I was unable to reach you on any level, and you shunned any comfort I offered. You even refused to believe the truth.'

She had failed, she reflected, caught up in her own grief, wanting so much to confide, to *believe*, but unable to summon the right words. So she'd chosen silence, attempting to adopt a normal façade at a time when life itself had been the antithesis of *normal*.

Would the tragedy have righted itself, given time?

Perhaps, she admitted silently. If it hadn't been for Sierra's meddling. If her belief in Raúl's fidelity hadn't been shaken.

Instead she'd allowed doubt and confusion to reign, influenced by what? The innuendo and lies of a bitterly disappointed woman who hadn't won what she considered to be the prize: Raúl Velez-Saldaña.

A shiver shook Gianna's slender frame. The fact Sierra had almost succeeded acted as a fist crashing into her heart.

If it hadn't been for Teresa's illness...

Would Raúl have used his persuasive power not to mention a degree of emotional blackmail to bring Gianna to fulfil Teresa's wish?

Gianna had refused once, too hurt and too stubborn to consider Raúl's avowal of truth.

If...*if* she'd filed for divorce, as she had thought to be the logical step to gain closure, would he have sought to dissuade her? Suggested a reconciliation?

Maybe not.

The realisation of how close she'd come to losing him almost crushed her.

Tears welled up in her eyes and threatened to spill.

'Don't.' It was a despairing groan dredged up from his soul, and he touched a gentle finger to her trembling lips. '*Don't*...please.'

Oh, God. Where did they go from here?

Her eyes met his, and locked, silently begging him to understand. How did one compensate for the loss of three years? So many days...more than a thousand nights.

Had he lain awake *aching* for her as she had for *him*, only him? Examining every word, every action, in vivid detail...and longing to go back and change some of those words.

She should have fought for him...fought for what they'd shared. What she'd believed they had together.

Instead she'd run, escaping to the other side of the world, *convinced* it was the right move, the *only* move she could make.

Refusing, in mindless agony, to listen to or condone his truth, because...*why*? There had seemed so many legitimate reasons at the time. And she'd been so emotionally distraught she hadn't listened to reason or thought it through...just acted *in anger*.

Had a similar degree of anger kept him away after he'd flown in to the Gold Coast to explain and attempt a reconciliation?

She had vivid recall of the words she'd flung at him in accusation.

'I tried so hard to believe you.' Her voice sounded husky, almost desperate.

'Not an easy ask, given Sierra's deliberate machinations.'

They'd come so far. Did she have the courage to take the next step and help bridge the gap?

It would mean baring her soul. *Vulnerable,* when she'd shored up her shattered heart and papered over the cracks.

Love was a four-letter word, but one of the hardest to say.

Yet hadn't she shown him with her body, with every touch, each caress…*dammit*, everything…how much he meant to her?

It wasn't merely intimacy, or *just* sex. Each time they made love it was *lovemaking*…the gift of body, heart, *soul*.

Tell him, an inner voice prompted.

Except she balked at voicing the words. For once she did the rest of her life, as she knew it, would change.

And she'd already *made* a new life for herself. One to which she'd sworn to return. Was *committed* to return. How could she renege on arrangements already in place?

Almost as if Raúl knew the passage of her thoughts, he cradled her head and closed his mouth over hers in a kiss that took hold of her heart and bound it to his own.

When at last he lifted his head, he traced light fingers over her full lips and smiled slightly as they trembled beneath his touch.

'You're not going anywhere, *mi hermosa*.'

She was willing to swear her heart tripped a beat. 'What are you saying?'

'I want you with me always. I believe it's what you want, too.'

Gianna wanted to give an unequivocal yes, for that was how she felt with her heart.

'I love you. I don't want to let you out of my sight. Whatever you need to tie up in Australia can be done from here.'

'I can't do that,' she said slowly. 'There's Bellissima…'

'Which is operating successfully without you. Appoint Annaliese as permanent manager. Assign her a percentage of the profits as an enticement.'

'My apartment…'

'Lease it out.'

'Jazz,' she offered in a strangled voice, and saw his eyes darken. 'My cat. He's currently in a boarding cattery.'

'We'll arrange to fly him here.'

Gianna sat upright. 'Raúl…' Whatever else she might have said trailed to a halt as she viewed him in silence. 'What exactly are you proposing?'

'Do you need to ask?'

'Yes. Yes, I do.'

'Our marriage resumed and reinstated. I want you with me every day, every night, for the rest of my life. As my wife. If Bellissima is so important to you, we'll source out a suitable boutique here.'

Stay? Remain here permanently? To be with him was what she wanted more than anything in the world…but she had obligations, responsibilities she needed to attend to, which meant a return to Australia.

She had to think with her head.

'A week. Just one week,' Gianna pleaded. 'I'll contact

Annaliese, call my lawyer, a leasing agent. Set everything in motion so it can be tied up as quickly as possible.' She placed a hand over her heart. 'I give you my word.'

'All of which can be achieved from here.'

'I have clothes, effects at the apartment I should take care of in person.'

'I can arrange for the entire contents of your apartment to be transported here, for cleaners to ready it for leasing.'

'Can't you *see*?' she begged. 'I *have* to go back.'

Her independence was something he admired. Together with her strength of purpose. Even in this instance, when it worked against him. If he could conceivably take a week and accompany her he would, but he had important meetings in Madrid all week, and in truth he was reluctant to be too far away from Teresa.

A week. It wasn't a lifetime. Capitulation at this point, given the big picture, their future together, wasn't an issue. Even if he'd merely exist without her.

'When do you want to leave?'

What was the time? Gianna checked the bedside clock. 'I can put a few calls through now. Follow them up with e-mails. I could probably take a flight within twenty-four hours.'

'I'll call my pilot and arrange to have the Lear jet on standby.'

'You don't need to do that.'

His eyes pierced hers. 'Yes, I do.'

Any further protest she might have voiced became lost as he stood easily to his feet, discarded his robe, then her own, and drew her down onto the bed and into his arms.

Telling Teresa of her plans wasn't the easiest thing Gianna had to do, but Teresa listened, nodded her head in silent agreement, and offered sagely, 'If you feel it's something you must attend to personally, then, my dear, you should follow your instinct.'

'A week. Then I'll be back.' She reached out and clasped Teresa's hands within her own. 'I give you my word.'

'I know,' she said gently. 'Raúl has made the necessary arrangements for you?'

'Yes.'

'When do you leave?'

'Late this afternoon.'

'Will you walk with me in the garden?'

'Of course.'

They talked only of the flowers, and how Miguel planned new borders for the spring, how splendid the colours would be…different shades of pink, lilac, dispersed among the white blooms. The brilliant yellows, creams…the reds in all their glory.

'I can visualise them now,' Teresa said wistfully. 'A glorious floral pathway. All my favourites.' She paused to offer a light laugh. 'I have so many.'

'You love it here.'

'Yes. My beloved husband brought me here not long after Raúl was born. He wanted to gift me something very special for the son we had made together. He thought this villa worthy of my attention,' Teresa revealed. 'I fell in love with it at first sight. The view was amazing, the interior perfect. It did need a little tender loving care, and that was given. I had *carte blanche,* and when it was finished we came here often. I designed the gardens, and now Miguel keeps them much the same. I am sure his hands itch at times to plan something different, but he never argues with me. Occasionally I feel inclined to surprise him, but that would mean change, and I prefer to keep things the way they were. It helps me remember the good times. The tree which Raúl loved to climb, until he fell and broke his arm. I wanted the tree cut down, but my husband insisted it should stand as a reminder.' She lifted a hand and indicated the tree. 'It beckons children, don't you think?'

Something caught in Gianna's throat, and she swallowed it down. 'Yes, it does.' In fact, its branches seemed to curve inwards, almost in a protective embrace.

'This place represents so much to me. Above all, it lends itself to peace. It's where I want to be…among so many wonderful memories.'

They had walked almost full circle, and as they re-entered the villa Teresa drew her close in a gentle hug. Gianna extracted the gift she'd bought and placed it in Teresa's hand.

'For you, with my love.'

'May I open it now?'

'Please.'

Teresa carefully undid the decorative bow, removed the ribbon, opened the jeweller's box, and her eyes shone with pleasure. 'Oh, my dear. It's exquisite. I shall treasure it. Thank you.' She lifted a hand and cradled Gianna's cheek.

'Soon you must ready yourself to leave. And I must rest. Travel carefully, my dear, and God speed. Above all, thank you for spending time with me.'

Any second now she was going to cry. 'I adore you.' They were the only words she could summon, and Teresa smiled gently.

'And I you.'

Gianna made it to the staircase, then her eyes blurred as the tears welled.

In an hour Miguel would drive her to the airport, where the Velez-Saldaña helicopter would transport her to Madrid, and then she'd board the Lear jet *en route* to the Gold Coast.

She was doing the right thing—tying up loose ends, ensuring everything she'd worked for over the past three years was settled to her personal satisfaction.

One week…what was *one week* in comparison to a lifetime?

Gianna sent Raúl a text message just prior to climbing into the helicopter. Another in Madrid, during the taxi ride to Barajas Airport.

It was as the driver entered the carriageway leading to the international terminal that doubt settled like a shroud and an inner voice cautioned, *What the hell do you think you're doing? Are you insane?*

She was almost there, for heaven's sake. Any minute soon the taxi would pull into the departures terminal, the driver would remove her bag, she'd pay him and head inside.

Except suddenly it seemed all wrong.

The taxi slid into its allotted bay, and the driver killed the engine.

OK, it was now or never. 'I'm sorry, I've changed my mind. Please take me back to the city.'

English, she could almost hear him think. *Never know what they're doing.*

'You are sure, *señora?*'

She was never more sure of anything in her life.

'Yes.' She gave him the address of the Velez-Saldaña conglomerate's headquarters, then sank back in her seat.

CHAPTER TWELVE

WHAT if she was wrong?

What if Raúl wasn't working late at his city office? Oh, God, *don't think*.

This is what you want, she reiterated silently as the taxi slid to a halt outside the entrance foyer of the tall office building.

'Wait…please,' Gianna instructed as she slid from the taxi's rear passenger seat and crossed to the security intercom system.

Simply press the security buzzer, wait for video recognition to gain entry, then walk to the bank of elevators—one step after the other. How difficult could it be?

Are you kidding?

Except the memory of his touch, the way he kissed her… She momentarily closed her eyes at the vivid recall of their lovemaking. It was more than sexual coupling…so much *more*.

Dammit, she uttered beneath her breath. *What are you waiting for?*

Do it.

For a long moment nothing happened, and despair swept through her body. She was about to turn back to the taxi when the security guard's voice issued with polite warmth.

'*Señora*, Señor Velez-Sandaña is currently at his apartment. You wish me to telephone ahead and relay you are on your way to see him?'

'No.' She nervously lifted a hand and tucked a stray tendril of hair behind one ear. 'No,' she reiterated. 'I'd prefer to surprise him.'

'Very well. *Buenos noches.*'

Traffic at this time of the evening flowed fairly freely, and Gianna was aware of increasing tension with every passing kilometre that closed the distance to Raúl's apartment complex.

You can do this. The silent affirmation strengthened her resolve, and when the taxi drew to a halt in the sweeping forecourt she paid the driver, added a generous tip, collected her bag, then crossed to the building's entrance.

The doorman greeted her, ushered her in to the foyer, where she summoned an elevator and keyed in the appropriate floor when she entered it. She took a deep, calming breath as the electronic doors slid closed.

Passage to the high floor was swift, and she crossed with measured steps to the solid double doors guarding entry to his luxury apartment.

Don't hesitate, a silent voice bade her. Simply press the door chimes… *And wait.*

For an anxious moment she wondered if he was in… maybe he'd chosen to dine out.

Then he was there, and he stood in the wide aperture, his dark hair rumpled as if he'd raked fingers through its length.

Wearing black trousers and a loose-fitting white cotton shirt unbuttoned almost to his waist, he bore a faintly piratical air…solemn, almost brooding, as his eyes seared her own.

'I didn't take the flight.' Nothing quite like stating the obvious, she decided with a measure of scepticism.

Raúl inclined his head. 'So the pilot told me. I've been raising hell trying to track down your movements.'

Oh, dear, she hadn't thought of that.

'I intended to,' she said with innate honesty.

'What stopped you?'

For a moment she just drank him in…the essence of who he was beneath the sophisticated façade…the man she loved beyond all else.

One word, just *one*. 'You.'

'Leaving was your decision.'

'The wrong one,' she managed simply, and saw his eyes darken.

For a moment she imagined he struggled with the power of speech.

Except this was *Raúl*…someone who could fell a person with just a *look*, a powerful man never known to be lost for a word in *any* situation.

He stood aside and gestured for her to enter…and she did, hearing the solid clunk as the double wooden doors slid shut, aware in her heart that there was no going back as she turned to face him.

Her gaze was steady, her eyes luminous with the strength of her emotions. 'I love you.'

Raúl closed his eyes, then opened them, blazing obsidian and flagrantly emotive as he lifted a hand and brushed light fingers over the soft curve of her lower lip.

'*Gracias de Dios*. I never thought to hear you say it again.'

The warmth of his smile almost melted her heart.

'I never stopped.' Anything else she might have said remained unuttered as he pressed her mouth closed, then lowered his head and angled his mouth over her own in a teasing salutation she returned in kind.

Together they indulged in a leisurely exploration, until the tasting wasn't enough, and Raúl held her head captive as he increased the pressure, sweeping her mouth with his tongue as he circled it with his own in a mating dance that would have only one end.

Unbidden, her hands slid beneath his shirt to explore the taut muscle and sinew covering his chest and ribs, before moving to push the gaping edges over his shoulders in an effort to dispense with the restriction as she sought one dark male nipple with her lips, alternately caressing and nibbling the pebbled nub with her tongue…and heard his faint groan as she rolled it between the edge of her teeth.

With a sense of desperation she pulled his shirt free from his trousers and dispensed with it, revelling in the satin smoothness of his skin as she shaped him with her hands.

'Too many clothes,' she declared in a voice she barely recognised as her own, and heard his soft laughter as she reached for his belt, unfastened it, then worked the zip fastener free.

He lowered his head and lightly nipped the vulnerable curve at the edge of her neck as he dispensed with her jacket and dealt with the buttons on her blouse.

The bra came next, and she uttered a faint gasp as he lifted her high against him and eased her thighs around his waist, held her there with one arm while he captured her head with the other…and covered her mouth with his own in a kiss that reached right down to her soul.

On some level she became aware of being carried, the almost silent click of a door closing, then he released her to stand before him.

'I should never have left,' Gianna said quietly, then fell

silent by the sheer expediency of Raúl pressing a finger to her lips.

'Later.' His mouth curved into a warm smile, and his eyes...so dark and liquid with desire. She couldn't think of a word to say. 'Later we talk.' He trailed light fingers over each cheek and traced the outline of her mouth. 'For now, I have plans.'

A faint bubble of laughter rose in her throat. 'You do?'

'*Sí.*' He brought her close, moulding the length of her body against his own so there could be no doubt as to the strength of his arousal.

She lifted her face to his, and her eyes held an impish light as she sought to tease. 'Isn't it a little early for bed?'

'I don't have *sleeping* in mind.'

'Good.' It was a matter of simple expediency to pull his head down to her own and take possession of his mouth. Although it soon became debatable who possessed *who* as the kiss became something else...hungry, increasingly urgent, intensely sexual.

What remained of their clothes was rapidly discarded, and Raúl tore the covers from the large bed, then tumbled them both down onto the sheets.

His powerful body loomed over her own as he braced his weight, then he sought the sensitive hollow at the base of her throat, savoured it, and traced a path across her collarbone before slipping to the soft swell of her breast, lingered there before gifting equal time to its twin.

A soft groan in protest whispered from her throat as he trailed his lips to her navel, dipping his tongue into the indentation and leisurely circling it before moving low over her taut belly.

Her fingers dug into the sheets as he reached the soft

vee guarding entrance to her feminine core, and her hips arched instinctively as he sought the sensitive clitoris, stroking it until she begged him to ease the pulsing ache deep within.

Except he was far from done, and she tossed her head from side to side as the pressure built to an unbearable crescendo… Then he sent her high in a shattering orgasm… again and again…until her body trembled beneath his touch.

It was then he trailed a tantalising slow path to her mouth, covering it with his own as he eased his length into the moist passage, inch by inch, felt the tightness as her muscles convulsed around him…and with one powerful thrust he surged in to the hilt, waited there, then withdrew, only to increase the pace until electrifying passion became all-consuming.

Incandescent, unleashed and incredibly primitive.

More, so much *more* than it was believed possible…a true meshing of body, mind and soul.

Only with Raúl for her there could be no other, and she thanked the deity for recognising that fact.

Her arms instinctively tightened their hold, and Raúl lifted his head, his eyes dark and slumbrous in the aftermath of passion, only to have them sharpen measurably.

'I hurt you? *Dios…*'

Gianna stilled anything further he might have uttered by pressing light fingers to his mouth as she offered a shaky smile. 'No.'

He brushed his knuckles gently down her cheek. 'What is it, *querida*? Tell me.'

Honesty…there could only be honesty between them now. 'The folly of almost losing you,' she said quietly, and felt the well of tears build behind her eyes. 'If it hadn't have

been for Teresa's illness...' She faltered to a halt as words
failed her.

It was just reaction, she qualified. Emotional overload.
Except there seemed no power on earth that could prevent
the spill of warm liquid tracing slow tracks down each
cheek.

He uttered a heartfelt groan as he soothed each rivulet
with gentle lips and held her close. 'Don't.'

Gianna offered a damp smile as she met his darkened
eyes. 'You're my world. Everything,' she vowed quietly.
'Without you, I merely exist.'

Raúl covered her mouth with his own in an exquisitely
gentle kiss that tore at her heartstrings. 'You imagine it's
any different for me?' He traced her soft slightly swollen lower lip. 'You, *querida*, only you. Always, from the
beginning. Never just sex. Lovemaking. My body...yours,
uniting in something so powerful, so incredibly beautiful...
unique.'

He took possession of her mouth, savoured the silky
inner tissue, then retreated to gently nibble her upper lip.
'Believe, *mi mujer*, you are the very air I breathe. *Mi vida*.
My life.'

It was well into the night before Raúl rose from the bed and
ran a bath, then he returned and scooped Gianna into his
arms and carried her through to the *en suite* bathroom.

Steam and foam aromatic with lightly scented essence
filled the air, and he brushed his lips to her temple as he
stepped into the capacious tub and settled her down between his thighs.

'Mmm, nice.' It was so *good* to lean back against him,
close her eyes, and enjoy his ministrations as he used a
sponge and began spreading scented foam across the top
of her shoulders. From there he slid to her breasts, each

peak still tender from his touch, then down over her belly to the intimate folds at the apex of her thighs…so acutely sensitive from his possession.

She felt his lips caress the edge of her neck simultaneously with his erotic exploration as he sought her swollen clitoris, stroking it with a feather-light touch. Heat spiralled through her body, and she arched against his palmed hand, seeking the solace he offered.

The aftermath of lovemaking filled her with a piercing sweetness…seductive, intensely sensuous, *bewitching*, she decided dreamily.

'I can almost hear you thinking.' His voice was husky, close to her ear.

Three years lost. Although she'd achieved much during that time. Dealt with her grief, grown as a person, developed the skill to view life…*her* life…from a different perspective

In one easy move Raúl turned her to face him, and he cupped her face and tilted it so their eyes met.

'No more shadows,' he said gently. 'We have the rest of our lives. Together we'll deal with whatever the years may hold.'

Amen, Gianna accorded silently as he lowered his head and laid his mouth over her own in a tender, evocative kiss that stirred her senses and made her ache for more.

'Bed, I think.' He released the bath plug and stood to his feet, then pulled her upright and wrapped a towel like a sarong beneath her arms before filching another, which he hitched at his waist. He brushed teasing fingers along the edge of her jaw. 'This time to sleep, hmm?'

It was heaven to slip naked between the sheets and to have him pull her close in against his body and splay one hand over her stomach while the other cupped her breast.

The emotional pain which had clouded her life was

gone, along with the doubts and indecision. Almost as if he knew, she felt his arms tighten and the light touch of his lips against the curve of her shoulder.

In years to come their three-year separation would count for nought—just a misplaced stitch in the fabric of their life. A slight imperfection as a reminder that nothing was ever perfect. A good marriage had trust as its foundation, faith and love…always *love*.

For a wistful moment she almost wanted to start over with a joyous celebration, clear of the lingering insecurities she'd harboured at their wedding.

'Want to share?'

How did he do that? It was dark, and she hadn't moved.

His soft chuckle curled round her heartstrings. 'Your heart just began beating a little faster.'

It was a spur-of-the-moment idea, but one that grew with every passing second. 'I need to think it through.'

A reaffirmation of their vows.

Held in the grounds of Teresa's villa.

An intimate gathering with just a few close friends to share the simple ceremony, followed by a celebratory dinner. It could be the one gift Teresa would treasure for the remainder of her life.

Simple wasn't going to happen, Gianna realised, as Teresa had embraced the idea with such enthusiasm no one…not even the nurse…had the heart to rein her in.

A new gown must be selected, a guest list assembled, and flowers… What did Gianna think of white roses for her bouquet?

Vast floral displays must grace the foyer, and exquisite hand-crafted lace was presented for approval to grace the bridal table—or did Gianna prefer the finest linen?

It was a delight to witness Teresa's pleasure as selections were made, decisions reached, a date settled. Invitations were printed and delivered by hand.

A few close friends became forty in the blink of an eye, and Teresa's smile, her light bubbly laugh, represented a loving memory that would remain with Gianna for the rest of her life.

The Velez-Saldaña name ensured every detail was accorded perfection. Teresa didn't need to step outside the villa for anything everyone came to her.

With one exception…Gianna's gown must be personally designed and fitted by the *vendeuse* of Teresa's choice. Style patterns, photographs, material swatches were despatched for approval, selections made and examined and discussed…until they discovered the ideal combination.

Consequently the villa became host to a whirl of activity…exhilarating, exciting, with Teresa in her element as everything began taking shape.

Alerting Ben with the news had brought expressed brotherly concern.

'Are you sure about this?'

There were no lingering doubts, not even one. 'Absolutely.'

'You've thought it through? The permanent move to Madrid? Giving up everything you have back home?'

'Yes.' There was no hesitation in her voice. 'Be happy for me, Ben.'

'My caution stems from seeing you brokenhearted and emotionally bereft after leaving Raúl three years ago. And knowing what it took for you to overcome it.'

'I've been able to prove Sierra invented a tissue of lies about the hotel incident three years ago,' she revealed quietly. 'If I'd taken the time to employ a thorough check, and not reacted with my heart instead of my head, if I'd *trusted*

Raúl's word…' She'd left the rest unsaid, and registered her brother's empathetic response.

'In that case, I couldn't be more pleased for you,' Ben assured her gently.

'Thank you.'

They'd talked for a while, catching up on mutual news before ending the call.

Next, there was Bellissima and Annaliese…whose initial reaction was, 'You're joking.'

'No. I'm perfectly serious.'

'You're remarrying your husband, you'll live in Spain, and you're offering me permanent management, with an increase in salary *and* a percentage of the profits?'

'You got it.'

'Wow.'

'Is that a *yes*?' Gianna teased, and heard a whoop by way of response.

'Yes.'

Next on the list… 'I don't suppose you'd be interested in leasing a furnished apartment at Main Beach?'

There was silence. '*Your* apartment?'

'That's the one.'

'I'm dreaming. This is just one of those *out there* dreams, isn't it? Any minute I'm going to wake up. OK, I'll play. How much rent would you be asking?'

'How much are you paying where you are?'

Annaliese named a figure, and Gianna adjusted it. 'Do you think you can manage that?'

'Yes!'

'Then we have a deal. I'll instruct my lawyer to draw up the paperwork, you check it with your lawyer, sign it, and courier it back to me.'

'Would you mind very much if I call you back and confirm this is *real*?'

'Do it. You have my cellphone number.'

'Thank you.'

Gianna cut the call, then glanced up as Raúl entered the bedroom following his shower. 'Done?'

'Annaliese is ringing back.'

At that moment her cellphone pealed and she picked up, chuckled a little at the husky uncertainty in Annaliese's voice before she reiterated the details. 'I'll e-mail you within the hour to confirm.'

'You won't regret this,' Annaliese vowed fervently. 'I'm unbelievably grateful. Did I already tell you this?'

Only three times. 'I'm also grateful it's going to be such a smooth transition.'

Following a few pleasantries, she ended the call, and rolled her shoulders

'Tired?'

She turned towards him. 'A little. It's been an exciting day.'

'Then let me see if I can ease some of the pressure, hmm?'

The warmth of his smile almost undid her, and she uttered a pleasurable sigh as he rested his hands on her shoulders and began to massage out the kinks, the stiffness.

It was late, and tomorrow would bring more of the same, with last-minute dress-fittings, various checks, helping Teresa field phone calls confirming guests' acceptances, a final consultation re the menu.

Somewhere in amongst all that Gianna needed Miguel to drive her to the elite jeweller in downtown Palma to collect the ring she intended to gift Raúl.

His hands felt so *good*, and she let her head drop forward as he eased the silk robe from her shoulders, then removed her sleep tank and slipped his hands beneath the elasticised waist of her cotton sleep trousers.

'This is easing pressure?'

'Admiring your body.'

'With your hands?'

'Initially,' he promised huskily, as he teased her lips with his own.

It was nice…better than *nice*. She closed her eyes and breathed him in, loving the way he shaped her body, lingering with erotic intent at each pleasure pulse. Sighed when he drew her down onto the bed and began trailing his lips to each breast in turn, savouring each taut peak before tracing a path to her waist, then low to gift her the most intimate kiss of all…lingering as he sought the sensitive folds and felt her response, the quickened breathing, the faint groan as she began to soar, and the cry when she reached her climax.

Afterwards she lay there, sated and complete. 'What about you?' she managed huskily, and saw his smile. 'Another time, *amante*,' he said gently as he gathered her close. 'Now you need to sleep.'

CHAPTER THIRTEEN

THE day the reaffirmation of vows was to be held involved a flurry of activity which began to subside around mid-afternoon, as everything came together beautifully beneath Teresa's direction.

The floral arrangements were a majestic attestation to skilled artistry, their placements superb in the large room Teresa had chosen to hold the ceremony. Chairs were meticulously lined in rows facing a table covered in white linen.

The catering firm duly arrived and were soon busy in the kitchen, while Elena, Teresa and Gianna made a final check of the formal dining room, where tables bore floral centerpieces and were set with exquisite crystal, bone china and silver flatware.

'It looks beautiful,' Gianna complimented as she gave Teresa a warm hug. 'Thank you.'

'My pleasure.' Teresa cradled her face, then pressed her lips gently to each of Gianna's cheeks in turn. 'Now, go upstairs and get ready.'

Her suite held her bridal gown, encased in its protective dress-bag, with stilettos placed precisely in readiness, while exquisite new underwear reposed on the bed.

A slim velvet jeweller's case was in clear sight, and she crossed the room and opened it with cautious fingers.

A stunning sapphire surrounded by diamonds on a delicate gold chain rested on a bed of white silk, and beside it were matching sapphire and diamond ear-studs.

The set Raúl had bid an astronomical amount for at the charity auction.

There was a card, and she picked it up with trembling fingers.

For my beautiful wife. All my love. Raúl.

Tears welled in her eyes, and she blinked rapidly to dispel them. She couldn't, *wouldn't* cry.

Shower, make-up, hair, then dress, she bade herself silently, and set about achieving all four before slipping her feet into the elegant ivory stilettos.

The gown was perfection, in ivory silk and lace crafted to enhance her slender curves, with three-quarter sleeves, a delicately scooped neckline.

With care she attached the ear-studs, fastened the pendant…then she did a final close check of her make-up and added the lightest touch of blusher.

Time to go She took a deep breath, soothed the faint onset of nerves, then collected the bouquet of tightly bunched white roses and walked to the head of the curved staircase to join Raúl at its base.

He stood tall and magnificently male, his muscular frame attired in a formal dark suit, crisp white shirt and silk tie.

The look on his face was something she'd hold fast in her heart for as long as she lived. *Love,* naked in all its facets. For her. Only her.

For a moment it seemed as if he rendered her boneless, then she offered a shaky smile, placed a hand on the balustrade and began to descend.

Teresa waited to one side, her features alive with happiness as Raúl took the stairs and met Gianna halfway, then caught hold of her hand and brought it to his lips.

Eyes as dark as sin captured and held her own. 'Beautiful,' he complimented huskily.

Everything faded into the periphery of her vision…the magnificent foyer, Teresa, *everything*.

There was only Raúl…the heart and essence of the man who would remain a constant throughout their life together…the electrifying knowledge that he was the other half of her soul…and that nothing, *no one*, would have the power to destroy what they shared.

'Thank you.' Quiet words that conveyed more, so much more than polite acknowledgement.

His mouth curved into a smile that transformed his features, and held her transfixed for several heart-stopping seconds as he sought her mouth with his own in a gentle evocative kiss that lingered a little too long…and left her with a delicious breathlessness she fought to control.

He trailed his lips over her cheek to hover at her ear. 'Ready to do this?'

Gianna had never been more sure of anything in her life. 'Yes.'

Raúl reached for her hand and threaded his fingers through her own as they descended the remaining stairs to the foyer, where Teresa came forward to embrace them both.

'Bless you,' Teresa said quietly, and blinked rapidly to dispel the threat of tears.

Raúl curved an arm around his mother's waist, and together the three of them crossed the foyer to the lounge, where a few close friends had gathered in the presence of a priest.

The formal reaffirmation took place—solemn words

delivered with meaningful intent—after which Raúl spoke his personal vows, his eyes never leaving Gianna's own.

Heartfelt words which brought the shimmer of tears as she struggled to contain her composure.

Time stood still and it seemed as if they were the only two people in the room, with everything coalescing into this single moment.

There were words she'd rehearsed in her mind, except they weren't the ones she uttered. Instead, she said what was in her heart…imprinted on her soul.

'I gift you my love,' she vowed quietly. 'Everything, for as long as I live…and beyond.'

Her eyes dilated as Raúl cradled her face between both hands and kissed her with such incredible gentleness every that nerve-end deep within burst into vibrant life.

It seemed an age before he released her, and she stood feeling faintly bemused as a few of the guests clapped their approval and broke into delighted laughter.

The priest's eyes twinkled as he blessed the rings, and Gianna's lips parted as Raúl slid a ring studded with diamonds onto her finger, followed it with a magnificent solitaire. Then he removed a ring from his suit pocket and slid it onto a finger on her right hand.

Her original wedding ring—the one she'd removed and handed to him this morning…the one he'd chosen for her to keep. The new rings on her left hand signified a new beginning.

Her heart lurched a little as his eyes seared her own, dark, slumbrous with emotion.

Its significance didn't escape her, and her eyes dilated as he took hold of her hands and brought both to his lips in a silent touching salutation, merging the past with the present, together with the promise of their future.

Then it was her turn to remove the circlet with its twin

row of diamonds she'd bought as her gift for him, and she followed his lead by placing the new ring on his left hand, before slipping his original wedding ring onto his right hand.

Two minds that thought as one.

'Eternity,' she vowed gently, and followed his action by lifting his hands to her lips.

His eyes darkened measurably as he drew her close and kissed her so gently it almost brought her to tears.

Everything after that seemed an anti-climax, as guests were offered champagne, and there were toasts and good wishes exchanged. Raúl and Gianna mingled until Teresa requested everyone transfer to the dining room.

Fine food graced several serving dishes set at the formal table.

The staff had excelled themselves, providing succulent offerings to tempt the most discerning epicurean.

Raúl was *there*—physically, mentally and emotionally connected to her in a way that made her heart sing. Evident in a look, a touch…almost as if they communicated without the need for words.

If she could mark her life by the number of *best* days, today ranked right at the top. For happiness, love, and a future filled with both.

Together, they would make it so.

A family with a child…*children*, Gianna amended, hugging the knowledge that the initial event might be closer than she'd anticipated.

Too soon, she cautioned silently. Much too soon to even confide the possibility. It had been an eventful few weeks… an understatement if ever there was one. Three days late with her monthly cycle didn't necessarily equate to what she hoped, *prayed* it might mean.

Nevertheless, she merely took a sip of champagne, and

stayed mainly with iced water. Did Raúl notice? Teresa? *Anyone?*

A wistful smile curved her lips as she pictured a little girl with blond curls being held in her father's arms…a baby boy with Raúl's dark eyes and the promise of growing in his father's image.

Life…their future…stretched out in front of them. The path an adventure filled with joy, laughter and love.

Above all…*love*.

The forever kind.

Gianna felt the light brush of Raúl's palm down her spine, and she spared him a soft sweet smile glimpsed the warmth apparent in his dark eyes, the silent question evident, and her lips widened with mischievous sensuality.

For one brief instant his eyes flared, and he leaned in close. 'Soon the evening will end; the guests will leave.' His hand slid up to gently cup her nape, and lingered there. 'Then you will be at my mercy.'

'Promise?'

'You need to ask?'

No, she didn't. Instead she placed a light hand on his thigh, felt the muscles flex beneath her fingers, and lightly trailed a path dangerously high before transferring it to her lap.

'Careful, *mi mujer*,' he warned gently.

'Always.'

It was eleven when Teresa's nurse appeared to escort her to bed. Teresa had coped well with the day's excitement, and although she dispensed with any concern for her well-being, eventually she was unable to disguise her tiredness and flagging energy.

The catering staff departed, the guests discreetly brought the evening to a close around midnight, and when the last guest had departed Gianna waited as Raúl set the locks in place and activated the security system.

Without a word he swept her into his arms and crossed the foyer to the staircase.

A faint laugh emerged from her lips. 'I can walk.' A verbal protest that had little basis in intent. She loved his strength, the security of muscle and sinew, his clean male smell, the elusive cologne he used.

His lips brushed the top of her head as he ascended the stairs. 'You'd deny me tradition?'

She knew she'd never deny him anything. 'I'd hate anything to diminish your...er...' She was hard pressed to contain the soft laughter threatening to escape her throat. 'Performance,' she finally managed as he reached the gallery and turned towards the guest wing.

It didn't, as he ably proved again and again through what remained of the night...only to tease her awake in the early-morning hours.

Afterwards he held her close and shaped her slender curves, soothing her rapid breathing as she rested against him.

'Is there anything you want to tell me?'

'Your libido isn't in question.'

Raúl lifted a quizzical eyebrow as he dropped a light kiss on her temple. 'It'll keep?'

Yes, it would.

'Rest, *querida*,' he bade her gently as he felt the sweet brush of her lips in silent acquiescence.

His, he vowed silently. *Beautiful* in mind and spirit.

More important to him than anything else in his world.

Something he would endorse every day for the rest of his life.

EPILOGUE

CASSANDRA TERESA VELEZ-SALDAÑA entered the world two weeks ahead of her due date. In a hurry to be born and exercising her lungs to full velocity, as her father commented as he cradled the pink-faced squalling infant before transferring his daughter to her mother's chest where, with a subsiding hiccup, she quieted and nestled comfortably.

Dark hair, exquisite features and a mind of her own, Raúl mused, when she protested volubly as a nurse tucked her into a crib and trundled it to the nursery.

'*Gracias di Dios.*' The words teased the tendrils of Gianna's hair as he spoke them close to her ear. 'My beautiful wife,' he said gently. '*Believe* you're the love of my life.'

They were words he reiterated often…words she never tired of hearing. Gianna smiled, and lifted a hand to lay it against his cheek. 'Same goes.'

HARLEQUIN Presents

Coming Next Month

from **Harlequin Presents® EXTRA.** Available October 12, 2010.

#121 POWERFUL GREEK, HOUSEKEEPER WIFE
Robyn Donald
The Greek Tycoons

#122 THE GOOD GREEK WIFE?
Kate Walker
The Greek Tycoons

#123 BOARDROOM RIVALS, BEDROOM FIREWORKS!
Kimberly Lang
Back in His Bed

#124 UNFINISHED BUSINESS WITH THE DUKE
Heidi Rice
Back in His Bed

Coming Next Month

from **Harlequin Presents®.** Available October 26, 2010.

#2951 THE PREGNANCY SHOCK
Lynne Graham
The Drakos Baby

#2952 SOPHIE AND THE SCORCHING SICILIAN
Kim Lawrence
The Balfour Brides

#2953 FALCO: THE DARK GUARDIAN
Sandra Marton
The Orsini Brothers

#2954 CHOSEN BY THE SHEIKH
Kim Lawrence and Lynn Raye Harris

#2955 THE SABBIDES SECRET BABY
Jacqueline Baird

#2956 CASTELLANO'S MISTRESS OF REVENGE
Melanie Milburne

See below for a sneak peek from
our inspirational line, Love Inspired® Suspense

Enjoy this heart-stopping excerpt from
RUNNING BLIND
by top author Shirlee McCoy,
available November 2010!

The mission trip to Mexico was supposed to be an adventure. But the thrill turns sour when Jenna Dougherty and her roommate Magdalena are kidnapped.

"It's okay. I'm here to help." The voice was as deep as the darkness, but Jenna Dougherty didn't believe the lie. She could do nothing but lie still as hands slid down her arms, felt the rope around her wrists.

"I'm going to use a knife to cut you free, Jenna. Hold still."

The cold blade of a knife pressed close to her head before her gag fell away.

"I—" she started, but her mouth was dry, and she could do nothing but suck in air.

"Shhh. Whatever needs to be said can be said when we're out of here." Nick spoke quietly, his hand gentle on her cheek. There and gone as he sliced through the ropes on her wrists and ankles.

He pulled her upright. "Come on. We may be on borrowed time."

"I can't leave my friend," Jenna rasped out.

"There's no one here. Just us."

"She has to be here." Jenna took a step away.

"There's no one here. Let's go before that changes."

"It's dark. Maybe if we find a light…"

"What did you say?"

"We need to turn on the light. I can't leave until I know that—"

"What can you see, Jenna?"

"Nothing."

"No shadows? No light?"

"No."

"It's broad daylight. There's light spilling in from the window I climbed in through. You can't see it?"

She went cold at his words.

"I can't see anything."

"You've got a nasty bruise on your forehead. Maybe that has something to do with it." His fingers traced the tender flesh on her forehead.

"It doesn't matter *how* it happened. I'm blind!"

Can Nick help Jenna find her friend or will chasing this trail have Jenna running blindly again into danger?

Find out in RUNNING BLIND, available in November 2010 only from Love Inspired Suspense.